Snakes in the Wild Oats

*Terry –
Thanks for
your ministry!*

[signature]

Snakes in the Wild Oats

Ken Wotherspoon

VANTAGE PRESS
New York

This is a work of fiction. Any similarity between the names and characters in this book and any real persons, living or dead, is purely coincidental.

FIRST EDITION

All rights reserved, including the right of reproduction in whole or in part in any form.

Copyright © 1974, 2008 by Ken Wotherspoon

Published by Vantage Press, Inc.
419 Park Ave. South, New York, New York 10016

Manufactured in the United States of America
ISBN: 978-0-533-16072-3

Library of Congress Catalog Card No.: 2008904939

0 9 8 7 6 5 4 3 2 1

to my parents
and the good folk around Melville
and to Shirley and the gang

TABLE OF CONTENTS

Snakes in the Wild Oats 1
Box Social Cruelty 7
Sex Education or Pornography 15
Pastor's Punch 23
When I Shot the Dog 33
Up the Elevator Shaft 43
Brotherly Love 55
Warm Rain and Uniforms 63
Stage Fright 73
Hailstones and Character 81
Hiram the Hired Man 89
The Eye of God and the Vanilla Bottle 99
Swimming Hole Hopes 109
Graduation 117

Snakes in the Wild Oats

SNAKES IN THE WILD OATS

There was already quite a bit of heat in the rays of the early morning sun as I ran the two miles to school. Each of us Grade eighters from Runneberg School wanted to be the first to arrive in the Banner Hall grounds at least an hour and a half before our teacher signalled the start of classes with the old wooden handled bell rung from the porch steps of the school in the adjacent yard. We would arrive out of puff and excited as the mists rose from the hollows and the meadow larks rang out their morning jubilation.

In the delicious morning, we had shaken off the groggy slumber stolen from the late hours of the night, the earlier part of which had been spent skulking around, inside and outside, the bouncing, rollicking dance hall. There was always so much to learn at those community dances where soldiers came from as far away as Yorkton to make time with the local girls; and farmers whose faces we knew conversed loudly in small groups with strangers to us who came from points as far away as twenty-five miles. Quiet, older neighbors talked earnestly about things like Social Credit and William Aberhart and his threat to the Liberals and C.C.F. and the problems of early seeding with late wild oat growth, while their younger colleagues got high, or pretended to, on someone's cache of home brew and exchanged borrowed cigarettes. Fist fights always ended the dance and we had to stay to the end to see who would draw the first blood and who would go home beaten and wounded.

With the dew glistening and sparkling on the quack grass at the edge of the heavy poplar bush along the west side of Banner Hall and with the dust finally settling on the leaves after the feeble honk of horn signalled the departure of the last car, the yards of Banner Hall and Runneberg School settled down for the brief hiatus between the remnants of the bi-monthly dance and the onslaught of the early morning school arrivers intent on their mission of curiosity and discovery.

There were, after all, mysteries to be solved from the night before. There were treasures to be discovered. With the dedication and excitement of archaeologists digging up signs and artifacts of past ages and appropriating these objects to specified times and cultural habits, we had a mission to fit the sometimes hidden and sometimes lost articles of the celebration of the night before with the cultural, religious and interpersonal lives of people we knew and of strangers who affected the lives of these people.

Would we find the body of the young soldier who got so drunk that he started flailing out at the one guy we knew you shouldn't pick on? It was right after the "beer-barrel polka" had its third run and the heavily-muscled farmer decked out in his new tweed suit was escorting his partner to a corner seat in the hall. The soldier intercepted, murmuring something about, "Whose fighting for this country anyway? Gimme that girl." When the Charles Atlas-built agriculturist grabbed the soldier by the arm and said, "Back off, drunken soldier boy, or you'll get winged before you see your first trench," the uniformed guy started his uncontrolled bellering with fists swinging. A couple of guys opened the corner door through which the farmer pitched the soldier as if he was a rag doll. Then he ran down the five steps and picked him up and beat the daylights out of him. We all thought it was a good show because we knew that strangers shouldn't come in like that and just because they wore uniforms shouldn't think they owned the place.

But we felt kind of bad when a couple of guys, I think they were the same two who opened the door, dragged the limp uniformed body into the deep brome grass at the edge of the bush north of the hall. We heard the body groan, and when the laughing, loud-talking group swayed back into the hall, we went up to see if he was alive. Then we got scared and ran around to the front of the hall. This bright sunny morning only showed a spot in the grass like you see when you come to a place where a deer slept the night before.

Then we had to check out Helen. Although she was a much older sister of four kids at school, she possessed a mysterious spirit that made her a legend amongst the members of the Grade 8 class. All five of us were boys.

Helen was old enough and big enough to live on her own. She had, it seemed to us, long since left her home and moved to Melville. That was a long distance of twelve miles from my home and ten miles from Runneberg. Especially in the winter. I remember it took my Dad and me most of the forenoon to go by closed-in cutter from our farm to town. It was during these all day excursions that a boy really got to know his father. In the privacy of the squeaking, squawking cutter with your backs freezing and your knees burning from the homemade barrel stove all sorts of understandings grew.

We didn't know what kind of work Helen did in town but we expected it would be a pretty high-class job because she really looked like a high-class girl. We kids saw her one time when she came to school to see Mr. Thompson, our teacher. I remember his handsome face turned red when she said she'd like to talk to him alone. I guess it had something to do with her younger brothers and sisters, likely some problem they'd been having and she came in place of her parents. Mr. Thompson was always a gentleman even in times of disciplining his flock. If he ever had to get mean for our sake he seemed to find it hard because he was so kind inside.

We supposed that he knew why Helen had come and he'd find it uncomfortable discussing teacher-pupil problems with such a beautiful and kind person as Helen. We sort of pretended to be working really hard on our map of the Hudson's Bay area when Helen stepped inside the room. But when we could tell from the whispering that they'd be outside, we took turns running up to Mr. Thompson and asked to leave the room. He didn't say he minded but he sort of looked annoyed at us Anyway it gave us a chance to see this femme fatale again.

She was almost as tall as our teacher. She had a fair complexion with dark eyes and long, straight black hair that hung well over her shoulders. So many ladies her age wore their hair in curls or piled up at the back, but a look at Helen's hair gave us boys a queer kind of internal sensation that we tried to talk about except it kept choking off the words in the back of our throats. She had fairly long legs. It's funny but, at least so we said to each other, we hadn't talked much or noticed much about legs until we passed Helen and caught a glimpse of them as we sped to the outside toilet to make good our excuse at bothering Mr. Thompson. She was standing with one of those legs sort of pointing out as if there had been a stone she was trying to touch with her toe. Her legs made us want to compare the legs of the skinny and fat girls in school. We used to bend way back and sort of scrunch down in our desks to look under the seats ahead, but there were no legs like Helen's. And there was no voice like hers. When she spoke and when she laughed it confirmed for us that she was particularly well-blessed with charm, personality and physique.

Helen always came to the dances, and she had been at this one. Because we had become more interested in her after her visit to the school and because of the queer feelings we had which we could hardly talk about after she left, we were more interested in her than even before. There were places to explore and thoughts to be shared about where Helen walked and visited and laughed and we wanted to relive these sounds and places before school started.

We human beings have certain basic drives and needs. Each generation copes as its social laws allows it to cope with these needs. Sometimes repression is the unsuccessful coping device because of cultural norms making expression difficult. Recognition of the dynamic at work gets twisted and distorted into all sorts of semi-secret practices and rather amusing diversions. But the drive goes on; it must release itself. Puritanical habits encourage illicit practices which can be as hurtful as the opposite pole where the social demon expresses its feelings and drives openly and flagrantly forgetting the slightest standards of human dignity. At Banner Hall youth grappled with initial sexual urges according to the norms of a tightly-fashioned moral environment. Helen would cut through the hypocritical veneer and let us see how some people coped as they would with the God-given sex drive.

Helen was at the dance before we guys even got together. She was wearing a black dress with lace that made her legs look like an illustration in Eaton's catalogue. We weren't sure how she got to the dance, nor did we care that much. She was there. And she was laughing and talking in that soft, melodic tone again. She was almost too light on her feet to be human, but we assumed that the work she did and the people she was with in Melville gave her a gracious air that only princesses and really privileged people could acquire. We got the impression that she knew everyone in the hall and when she spoke to the noisy couples and singles coming in the door she greeted them as if she was the hostess at a grand ball. The other ladies, although well-dressed, bathed and perfumed for the evening looked used and tired in comparison. They didn't give us the feeling that they knew her as well as she knew them; in fact, they seemed rude to her and almost acted like they thought they were of superior birth or something. Some of them didn't even respond to her greeting. I guess there's no worse way to treat a person like Helen than to pretend she wasn't there. The men, however, were something else. We guys had to talk about that a bit. We noticed that they seemed glad to see Helen, although the guys with wives or girlfriends beside them turned a little red like Mr. Thompson. But the guys who came in alone, the stag line, were really great. They shouted a loud and friendly greeting back to Helen; some of them even marched right up beside her and gave her a kind of pat on her tightly-shaped behind. They say it's good to show your concern for people by expressing it through a touch or an act. Helen sure seemed to appreciate it.

We kept noticing that as the dance got going, Helen kept going outside with these different guys, especially the friendly ones. We assumed at first that it was because they would sneak out behind the bush or behind a row of cars in the dark and take a quick snort out of a bottle. But after investigating these groups, which got louder every time they came in and went out again until the two Mounties came and scared them with their flashlights, we noticed that Helen and whoever she went out with didn't go into these groups. We noticed, too, that even though Helen looked a little more tired each time she came back in, she didn't get noisier and drunker like the other people. So we decided to follow her and her companion out and watch where they went.

It was a surprise to us that the couple walked rather briskly through the parked car area, past the noisy clusters and drinkers and the politicking conversationalist; to an area right beside Reid's wheat field where a single car was parked. They got into this car but we couldn't see what they were doing nor could we hear what they were saying. We could only hear a man's voice which seemed to get lower and lower and Helen's delicious laughter. Tiptoeing to the back window of the car we almost got caught when the door opened and two people practically tumbled to the ground beside the car. It looked so funny to see Helen and her friend acting like a couple of little kids, giggling and rolling under the fence into the growth in the field. We thought we'd better hike on out of reach before they saw us and asked us to play with them. And we marked the spot in our memories for early exploration in the morning.

You can imagine our fascination as we ran across the soft ball field, past the chirping crickets, scaring startled gophers into their holes, to the two-stranded barbed wire fence protecting the luscious growth of the new crop in Reid's field. In the hollow between two sloping knolls where the wild oats was growing way faster than the wheat, the crumpled stems of the new growth were mashed together in a dozen different spots where lovely Helen had a dozen different games like the one we started to watch. And thrown around the ground like spent balloons after a child's birthday party were the elongated remains of the prophylactics, which, as we were to learn later from older boys, insured Helen's lithe figure and her friends' reputation. One of us commented, "Look, snakes in the wild oats!"

BOX SOCIAL CRUELTY

Community dances may have been facilitative in the socializing process in the forties on the prairies, but for sheer status-seeking amongst the female set there was nothing that could match the Banner Hall box social. Wall-flowers may have had their origin at the dance and girls could feel the crushing weight of loneliness and rejection creeping up on them when left to the last by the local swain in a schottische or a moonlight waltz, but if at a box social, your contribution received the lowest bid, or worse still, was left in the surplus pile when the bidding was finished, that spelled humiliating defeat. No one ever said so publically, but the young lady who had to sit by herself and consume her goodies when there were no bidders left must have felt in one night all the depression a paranoid feels in a year.

The knowledge that the boxes were unmarked as to the donor's identity and hence had an aura of anonymity about them, hypothetically proving everyone's equality at box socials, did not really make the loser feel any better. It was a token attempt at constructing a rationale that didn't actually hold up when the nitty-gritty issues were faced. After all, the varying artistic abilities of the young ladies in the community were not so dissimilar and the numbers of entries were not so plentiful that the diversities in wrappings and ribbons along with the giggles that attended the elevating of the box in the auctioneer's hands could possibly keep the donor's identity a secret. We all knew who owned each box even though we pretended, even we five Grade eight boys, that it was a great surprise when the last bid was in and the apple-cheeked young lady claimed her box and her partner for the evening.

For the uninitiated in this aspect of prairie folklore let me summarize the philosophy and modus operandi of this peculiar prairie practice. In preparation for a box social, the single ladies of assorted ages and physiques and personalities would pack in a box a lunch for two. It might contain a couple of pieces of cake or pie that she baked, some sandwiches made with homebaked bread and cheese or eggs and maybe an original delicacy of her own favorite recipe. The box was then wrapped in colorful paper, if such was available, or paper she had colored herself, and tied decoratively with a ribbon. When she entered the hall she would unobtrusively remove the package from a brown bag behind a table so that the men who came to bid on the boxes supposedly could not associate the box with its giggling, wishful and slightly embarrassed creator. Then there might be a school program or some community singing or a lantern slide or a speech by the local delegate to the Wheat Pool or some other such educational event where everyone sort of acted as if they'd forgotten about the prospects of the matchmaking program that really highlighted the evening. This occurred when the auctioneer, usually Mr. Thompson our teacher, stepped to the table behind which the boxes were piled, pushed the table aside, and exclaimed at how beautifully wrapped these boxes were and suggested that the exterior of the packages were far less glamorous than the lovely young lady who prepared the tasty contents. Then he would briefly explain the procedure that the gentleman who made the final bid on a box would be the fortunate person to accompany box and owner to a corner table where the delicious lunch would be shared by the couple. Then they would act as a couple for the dance that followed. And all of us knew this could be the beginning of a romance pre-designed in heaven or it could be the worst ordeal of the season for either one of the parties. However it turned out, it meant that we guys in Grade eight would end up eating a scrumptious lunch with the ladies whose boxes were left over when the supply of male bidders ran out. Mr. Thompson was the kind of person who made this last act a little less humiliating by joking with the surplus ladies and kidding us kids on how we came to these events simply because we wanted to eat. Anyway, that's the way it appeared to the five of us.

The other boys and I noticed that Gus was late for the educational event preceding the box social. We whispered about this as we huddled together on a bench at the back of the group. We hoped he'd be there for the social because he usually was the life of the party particularly if he gave off a very pungent odor when he came in. This meant that he had been experimenting again, as our parents explained it to us, in some project on a medicine that might really clear him of his many ailments. We surmised that Gus was likely detained in his lab. Without him the bids would not go very high because when Gus got in a playful mood he would keep pushing up the bids and he seemed to know when to quit so that the other guys got the last word in and had to buy the box.

The voice of the man from the Wheat Pool began to quaver as his growing nervousness began to affect his vocal chords. This was no doubt due to the fact that he understood his subject much better than he appreciated having to tell his audience about it. It was a cruel joke amongst us five that we'd guess how long he

BOX SOCIAL CRUELTY

would talk with fiery enthusiasm before his voice began to break and he'd begin to fidget and get uncomfortably red behind his ears and greenish under his eyes. With one "big ben" pocket watch amongst us we'd place little non-payable bets on the time. If a speech that lasted say one hour could go beyond fifteen minutes before he'd begin the breaking-up process, that was usually pretty good. Once his voice started to rise in pitch and shake tremulously it was kind of pathetic. He looked as if he'd like to drop through the furnace register or run outside bawling. But being a man and a really good citizen to boot made him the victim of oratorical injustice. We would always hope that he could keep going without starting to cry, but we'd giggle nevertheless. Tonight he got through twenty-five minutes before the old villain stage fright caught up to him again. But the problems of wheat delivery and farmer co-operation would own the stage for another forty tortured minutes. Suddenly the main door of Banner Hall flew open and a hearty "Whash goin' on? Whate' we waitin' for!?" announced Gus' arrival. His lab experiments had gone really well that day.

 He was a great guy. He loved kids. The fellow from the Wheat Pool drew a quick and relieved conclusion to his speech as Gus came up to our bench, lifted it up from the end and slid all five of us exclaiming "Don't do it, Gus!" to the floor. As I was getting up I caught a glimpse of my mother who with Dad, sat ahead of us with some of the other married folk who were here not for the box social but the event that was just ending. She gave me that look of disapproving reprimand that didn't require words to drive its point home. I was not to encourage Gus in his attempts to break up a serious meeting in order to get on to the more frivolous entertainment of the evening.

 Gus' triumphal entry did make its point. The speaker for the evening was thanked and everybody clapped. Gus meanwhile seated himself on a bench next to us as our parents and the other married couples put on their coats to leave. I noticed that Gus seemed to find the hot air in the room too much contrast to the frosty air he had just left and his eyes sort of glazed over as if he was about to fall asleep. This gave me a chance to look at him more closely.

 He must have had a very heavy day in his lab because his whiskers bristled out like my dad's did when he got too busy to shave for a couple of days. Also, he hadn't taken the time to dress up for the box social. He wore heavy blue cover-alls over another pair of G.W.G. pants the cuffs of which hung below the cover-alls. His mackinaw was unbuttoned but he hadn't removed it despite the growing heat in the room. His black woollen cap hung limply over his left knee, and when he pulled it off his head it left his hair hanging in all directions. He looked just like the kind of fellow my mother told me I'd be if I didn't keep myself neat. But this rough exterior couldn't hide the real Gus. We boys knew that he had the heart of a fairy godmother. He always played with us kids when he came to the schoolyard at recess time. We figured that he was still a bachelor because no girl had been born who could match his kindness and gentleness. I remember one time when he helped my older brothers load a pig into a wagon. The pig wouldn't go where he was supposed to and my mean brothers started prodding it with a pitch fork causing the pig to jump ahead while releasing earth-shattering squeals. Gus was a big man. He grabbed the pitch fork without scolding anyone, threw it against the barn and wrapped his massive arms around the pig's neck literally hugging the animal up the ramp and into the wagon.

He was probably a very shy person. When he met us and took time to play ball with us or something, he didn't make a lot of fuss or noise like he did when he came to dances or box socials after working hard on his medicines. Maybe he needed the extra energy he got when he experimented to help him face people in crowds. Anyway the crowd wasn't bothering Gus tonight.

Most of the men sat on one side of the hall and the girls whispered to one another in groups of two or three along the benches on the other side. We stayed on our bench not too far from Gus. Mr. Thompson began the ritual from the front of the room just to one side of the giant grate that let the hot air fly upwards from the furnace in the basement.

"And now for some fun and fellowship", announced Mr. Thompson. "These decoratively adorned boxes are hardly matched by the beauty of the young ladies who spent hours preparing them for the lovely lunch we're going to enjoy later tonight. I know that you young fellows would like to buy them all, but, of course, the rules are one box to a bidder. And that's the way the game is played. Let's be fair in our bidding and generous in our offers. The money, as you know, is going to help in the work of the Red Cross. There's no charity more worthy of your active involvement." The five of us all nodded knowingly at each other. We were all badge-wearing members of Runneberg School's Junior Red Cross Society.

"Now let's get on with the action. As you know, tonight's box social will end with a dance, so let's try to get a partner for everybody tonight. And, as we know, so many of our young men are away fighting for our King and our country, it may mean that some young ladies will have to pool their boxes with those of us who won't be bidding. Just remember, if you should be such a young lady, your box is no

BOX SOCIAL CRUELTY

less beautiful than the others and, of course, the fact that it may be left over in no way reflects on you as a person. I don't even have to remind you of that because as you know, the anonymity of each person has been carefully safeguarded by the rules which have been set out by the Banner Hall Board of Trustees regarding the handling of box socials."

"Letsh get on with it!" Gus had revived a bit from his half slumbers. I thought he might have restrained himself a little; after all, Mr. Thompson was only safeguarding the feelings of some of those women we guys knew were going to be hurt again. He was the kindest of all the men in the district, including Gus, and he knew in his heart about the hurts those girls felt. Anonymity and hidden identity be damned, someone had to be left out and it usually turned out to be the same ones.

However, Gus' unsolicited reprimand from the floor got the proceedings moving. Mr. Thompson now was very much aware of Gus' presence, but Gus seemed to be more and more oblivious of Mr. Thompson and the rest of what was going on that evening. He still had his mackinaw on and he kind of slouched forward as if he was getting ready for a fight or something. "C'mon, letsh get on with this aucshion!" he bellowed. His words slurred badly. I noticed that the other four guys were all leaning forward looking at Gus, too.

Mr. Thompson selected a brightly bedecked box from the pile and held it above his head. "What a masterpiece of creative genius," he began. "Think of the hours of labor expended on this beauty, not to mention the work of designing it in the first place. I know just by the feel of this one that it's cram full of the sweetest cake and the most scrumptious sandwiches. And it belongs to one of those lovely young ladies out there," he pointed to his right at the giggling women, one of whom had turned scarlet from the top of her blouse up to her hair. We thought that he was laying it on a little heavier than usual. He kept looking nervously towards Gus, who was by now raising his right hand in the air and shouting, "Five!"

"Excuse me, sir, five what?" gently interjected Mr. Thompson.

"Five!" rejoined the impatient and wavering Gus. "Five! Letsh get going!"

This interchange repeated itself at least three times before one of the other men in the group got Mr. Thompson off the hook by shouting, "We'll call it 5 cents. I'll bid 10!" Us kids exchanged disgusted glances as the other men joined their colleague in rolls of derisive laughter, slapping the new bidder on the back and pointing their thumbs back over their shoulders towards the now obnoxious Gus. "Five!" he blared again, his eyes breaking through the glaze I noticed earlier into two miniature sparkling fire balls. "Five!"

Mr. Thompson uneasily announced his interpretation that the bid was being raised by five cents. This action repeated itself until Mr. Thompson remembering how the formerly good-natured Gus would allow his competitor the last bid, shouted "Sold to Bill Hadlubech for two dollars and fifteen cents!" That was an enormous price to pay for a box. A slightly crest-fallen Bill Hadlubech rose and went forward to pick up his newly-acquired box and match it with his blushing hostess for the evening.

The auction continued in this vein until the last male bidder had paid out his hard-earned cash and the surplus boxes were set up on the table for the ladies who prepared them to pick up and begin pooling the residue. The unique thing about this box social that we five had never witnessed before was that because Gus kept shouting "Five!" everytime a box went on the auction block, every box that got bid on was sold on a first come, first serve basis. This eliminated that cruel process of having to set some gal's box down with no bids on it and going on to another. Tonight the ones who got left over knew they were left over simply because there were no men left to bid on them. Except Gus.

By this time Gus was beyond bidding anything. The number five that stuck with him through the bidding had now miraculously left him before he got the opportunity to claim a box for himself. I'm sure the remaining ladies prayed for this miracle and became devout believers when it occurred.

Gus' feet slipped forward to the point that his felt socks lost their grip on the floor, the bench started leaning back and we kids just began to smother the squeals of delight from our mouths when over he went sprawling across the floor. His heavy body literally caused the bench to squirt forward into the bench ahead of him and he rolled over on his side with a loud groan and heaved out a dying "Five" before he went into a deep sleep. Gus' medicine took its full measure.

It's amazing how people learn the art of ignoring unpleasant scenes. Middleclass tourists in India or Brazil can happily walk by the outstretched begging hands of little hungry children; busy shoppers obliviously walk by the appeals of charitable organizations and urban-dwellers can conveniently overlook the needs of their next door neighbors saying that they didn't know. In Banner Hall, one of the neighbors with a severe drinking problem got conveniently left there in the middle of that floor while the lunch end of the box social went on. Nobody seemed to remember that Gus had come. No one appeared grateful that it was his bidding that made the social such an overwhelming success financially and bids contributed so much to the cause of human dignity.

BOX SOCIAL CRUELTY

But Gus' resources ran deeper than those who now ignored him. He had a secret weapon.

When it came to having to mind to one's physical needs such as relieving yourself, at Banner Hall, the women went to the outdoor toilet at the end of a path in the bush west of the hall and the men walked into the darkness in the parking lot. Now Gus had the same spiritual and physical needs as anyone else. Even his drunken sleep could not block the expression of the need to relieve himself of the heavily filled bladder that resulted from his hours of consuming the home brew he was so talented at making. A loud clicking sound from his teeth that resulted from Gus clamping hard on his gums to offset the heavy downward pressure from his bladder should have alerted some of the male adults to his problem. But everyone, except a couple of us kids who stood beside Gus as we munched into cake swamped in heavy icing, expediently ignored Gus' plight.

Out of his drunken stupor he summoned a hint of control over a limp arm that lifted itself and then fell to the floor. The movement recurred three or four times until his sluggish, pawing fingers found their way into the folds of the fly of his coveralls. A tired but desperate tug caused a couple of buttons to fly across the floor; he lunged in at the fly again and got hold of the old G.W.G.'s next to the heavy woollen underwear which in turn were next to the elongated fleshy object that he was searching for. With a tug on these remaining garments and a groan of nightmare despair he flipped himself over on his side and pulled out what us boys considered was more instrument than we saw when Reid's holstein bull mounted a cow. This he held between two fingers and now with a subsiding groan that was truly a sigh of relief began to flood the polished floor boards of Banner Hall.

Pandemonium broke loose. Women jumped to their feet upsetting the benches where they'd been eating the box lunch with their partners; men feigned surprise, shocked expressions ready to avenge their ladies' intruder. Like true knights the men ordered the ladies to the basement as if to save them from humiliation and loss of dignity. The five of us noticed, however, that as these shattered damsels were escorted from the room, some of them protected their faces with their hands as if to shield their eyes but, we noticed spread their fingers in such a manner to allow an unobstructed glimpse of Gus' private equipment as they stampeded, squealing, from the room.

Gus had truly found relief. He lapsed once again into a deep sleep. A surge of sorrow and compassion for our friend saturated us as we saw the local heroes engage in a little cruel play at his expense. Grabbing him by his felt socks and his arms they proceeded to spin him in a clockwise fashion until his coveralls, his mackinaw and all his undergarments soaked up the urine he had so generously spilled across the floor. Then with loud bullying guffaws they pulled him into a corner and left him to waken sometime the next morning in a hangover that would be accompanied by feelings of shame, loneliness and bewilderment. And his clothes would stink, we thought.

And the dance after the box social went on.

SEX EDUCATION OR PORNOGRAPHY

I can't recall ever hearing the word "censorship" amongst the social groupings and cultural circles of the Banner Hall community. I have reason to recall, however, that the protectors of righteousness imposed an effective but informally regulated code of ethics upon those who would instigate amongst the innocent and naive a desire to read material that would encourage traders in pornography.

The "travelling library" was an institution of the early forties that attempted to meet the literary needs of the local farmers, supplementing the sparsely-supplied school library. Each month as that portable bookcase, resembling a large treasure chest, arrived and was unlocked by Mr. Thompson, we kids gathered around to experience the thrill that ran through us as we gasped in wonder at the bright red, green or blue jackets of the fresh array of books. Books always have a way of arousing the sense of wonder and discovery like rows of so many doors beckoning the curiosity of the beholder to knock, open and enter worlds whose mysteries are there to be experienced and solved.

The books were divided according to subjects and were separated on those little shelves into adult and children's books. The carefully-guarded morality of our homes and the explicit directions on the box cover combined to re-inforce the impression that these were books we kids just did not read. On one occasion only did I select an enticing sounding title from the fiction section of the adult books, only to discover that my parents' teaching was enthusiastically supported by my teacher's supervision of the only access I had to literature that told of unseen worlds. Taking the larger than usual book to Mr. Thompson's desk, I waited as he scribbled title and author on the little green slip that remained as the librarian's record of the borrowed book. He looked up at me with pencil poised over the borrower's name line and asked if this was for my Dad or my oldest brother, Les. Pre-conditioned about honesty by example and directive I had no choice but to blurt out, "It's for me." Mr. Thompson in his kind and empathetic manner, gently chastised me for not heeding the directions on the box that indicated I had chosen a book from the wrong section. The book was restored to its place in the gap between two leaning novels. My attempt at entering the adult world of human sexual encounter was to be suppressed for a while. But my curiosity received a new charge of determination. It would be fed by other sources.

I guess kids who grow up on farms where livestock are born, fed and sold to the cattle buyers have one direct source of sex education denied to our counterparts in the prairie towns and cities. Even if our parents told us at an early age that calves were born out of straw piles and colts just walked out of the woods, the direct exposure farm kids had with cows, bulls and horses soon dissipated the myths. After all, why did old Mr. Stalmbeck who lived near Crescent Lake, twelve miles east of our farm, never appear until that time of the year when our mares galloped restlessly to and fro in the pasture? He would come in a buggy which trailed a huge stallion and after some preliminary conversation my father would direct him to the pasture where the mares were kept. For an hour or two the stallion played games with the mares which looked like the early stages of leap frog. Then Mr. Stalmbeck would tie his stud to the buggy again and after extracting some dollar bills from my Dad would go on his way. We wouldn't see him or his stallion again for maybe a year.

And of course there was the more direct association we witnessed between our own bull and the heifers of our herd. There was the energetic and playful romp between the roosters and the hens in our flock of barred rock chickens. And, sometimes in the early spring the miracle of the birth of a calf took place before our very eyes as the rising mists of a new day enshrouded the cow as she encouraged the little fellow to pull himself out of the womb and then licked him clean with her own tongue and gently nudged him to stand on his quivering legs. The cycle of physical attraction, fulfillment and propagation amongst the horses and cattle and poultry to which we felt a kind of natural kinship soon dispelled any myths in our minds about the relationship between male and female in the animal kingdom. But how all of this applied to the relationship between men and women was left to other teachers. Sex education in the schools wasn't even thought of, I guess, certainly it wasn't spoken of. Parents did not speak of the subject except perhaps via remote allusions and references to the birds and animals without completing the association with the human level. Older brothers, of course, were extremely knowing and wise. At least they were generous in making references to some colleague who got his girl "in trouble" as they put it and "had to marry her." Even though we Grade eighters had difficulty completing the picture in our minds we knew it had something to do with acting married in some situations involving human relationships when actually you weren't.

Older brothers and their friends, it seemed to us, spent a lot of time at dances or outside the school at whist drives drawing on deep resources of shared pleasure as they told stories we hardly ever understood. Their loud guffaws always seemed to come at the point in the story where we five guys would be about ready to interject a comment like "What does that mean?" or "How come?" This made us sort of annoyed with our older brothers, because they treated us like kids. Maybe, it seemed to us, they didn't really know as much about the subject as they pretended and so they made jokes about it and laughed loudly at the place in the story where they felt most ignorant. Anyway they put up a good front. And for us kids we had to rely on helpful men like Corny to round out our education.

Corny rented a farm not far down the road from our place. If I wanted to take the long way to school I could go past his gate. Most of the time, though, I followed the path to school across the fields where we kids pulled out the growing crop to mark the path better and tramped down the brittle stubble on the land which was left to be summerfallowed. On the way back from school so that we'd have more time together before separating to get to our own homes and be faced with a list of chores that had to be completed before supper time, we'd often follow the graded road that led by Corny's farm.

I guess Corny wasn't a very good farmer. He seemed to spend a lot of time visiting around during the hot days when most men would be sweating it out behind a set of harrows drawn by an outfit of horses or picking stones from the summerfallow or hauling grain or water or something. He always got his crops in but there were more wild oats and sowthistle than grain. In fact, I remember in the company of my brothers and sisters pulling the blooming mustard plants from our grain when the wheat was in the shot blade and seeing in the distance Corny's field bright yellow like the rape crops of today but infested with the weed we were controlling in this primitive but effective manner. Dad always insisted it was guys like Corny that made our labor more difficult because the flowing creeks and winds would carry the infectious seeds from the weeds in his field.

But if Corny failed in agricultural expertise he excelled in what he called "making women". That term, the first time we Grade eighters heard it, conjured up pictures in our minds of a man busily engaged in the art of constructing wax figures of assorted female human beings. Unlike our parents and our teacher, however, Corny used a more direct method of dealing with the natural curiosity of early adolescents. When we asked him to explain how he made women he expressed surprise that we didn't know. Right then and there on a hot afternoon in June we sat down on the green grass on the side of the road not far from Banner Hall and with Corny as our teacher got a straightforward, uninhibited and illustrated lesson in sex education.

Corny was the community Casanova. He was about five and a half feet tall with black wavy hair and a tanned face that always displayed a boyish grin. Every woman must have wanted him as her pet because he looked innocent and friendly at the same time. He was usually in the company of different girls when he was out and he seemed to be very gallant and gracious with them. He liked to wear brightly colored ties when he was at the dances, which made him stand apart from the other men. His infectious smile and gentle laugh seemed to make people relaxed in his company. He spoke easily and rather fast.

To be bombarded with a great quantity of emotionally-charged information by a teacher skilled in an art he enjoyed so much that he literally perspired not from the heat of the day as by the anticipation of his own discourse, makes it difficult to assimilate all at once. We were naturally a bit dumfounded by Corny's depth of understanding and dedication to his subject. He was emotionally involved to the point that it was difficult to interrupt him with questions. It was as if he almost forgot who was in his class and went on as if he had a big subject to cover and time placed limitations on his delivery.

Corny believed in the teaching method that integrated enthusiasm of delivery with clear audio articulation and good video illustrations. He was not like teachers who believed that learning is a remote objective process of passing hard information from a knowledgeable teacher to an uninformed student; his pupils were seen as eager learners along with a teacher who was still learning. Motivation for research would ensue because of experiential first-hand telling by the central resource person, the teacher. In this case, Corny had a captive class, open and willing to delve into the subject he had brilliantly mastered.

"You guys know that girls aren't just different from boys," he began. "Don't tell me that you haven't learned more than that. They're different in looks, that is, they're built different on the outside and they're built that way because of what's on the inside. And what's on the inside is what we're most interested in because that's what it's all about. You see, when I make a woman I'm doing her a favor because I'm putting into her what she wants more than anything else in the world and if she doesn't get it, she's a screwed-up unscrewed woman, a nervous wreck."

The five of us just sort of looked at each other. We couldn't integrate all of this new information that quickly but none of us seemed quick enough or alert enough to ask for a more detailed retelling with pauses for reflection and questions. Such as what did he mean by "screwed-up" and all that? Corny anticipated this I guess because he paused and took from his overall pocket a worn, black, leatherbound book that resembled a notebook or an address book. He opened it and extracted a tattered photograph which he set on the grass in the middle of our huddled group.

The photo was of a naked woman. I had never in all my youthful days, imagined that a woman could, in fact, look so different than a man. I can recall thinking how strange it was that I didn't seem interested in her face. Faces of people always seemed so important. You looked for the marks of character in a person's face. Everyone has his own face. The nose is either pronounced and aggressive or withdrawn and ashamed of itself. The eyes of each person tells something about what he feels; they call you to come closer and take a better look and entice you to stay and get to know the person better or they turn you away and make you wish you hadn't looked in the first place. The mouth may be a channel for exchanging words, but it also says so much about the immediate feelings of an individual. If the lips open with the promise of a smile, it means stick around and let's talk. If they turn down or quiver a bit, it means go away, I'm scared or I don't like you. The face of a person tells you so much, I thought. To get to know a face is to know the person. But I couldn't remember or didn't want to look at this woman's face.

I suppose it was because there was so much more of her to see. I gulped as I viewed those breasts that needed no added adornment to make them any more pronounced. My eyes moved from these down to the narrow waistline, around the curvacious hips. And at the base of the flatness of her stomach the patch of hair that surprised me. We had never encountered anything quite like this before. Her shapely legs parted gently at the bottom of the triangular hair growth. They seemed very long.

Corny didn't say much as we picked the picture up and passed it from hand to hand studying it like a botanist might view a plant species he had never heard of before. There was a long reverent silence. Sparrows hopped frivolously in the maple trees inside Corny's gate and chirped happily, shielded by the shade from the hot early summer sun. Two gophers ran across the dusty road, one in hot pursuit of the other. In the distance a couple of crows cawed to each other. But we were speechless as we tried to drink in all this new information and sort out our emotional predicament of the last few minutes.

"Is it somebody from around here?", finally the questioner broke the stupor of his classmates. What other comment could we make? Corny's answer reinforced his earlier presuppositions. "Boys, I'll tell you something. She's from around here. You all know her. You see, she's a woman. Not some strange goddess or a princess from a far country, she's well known by all of you as the girl who sits ahead of you at school, or the girl you saw at the dance last Friday, or the girl just down the road here. Boys, you haven't begun to learn anything about life until you know this woman. Even if you get 81 in geography and 92 in arithmetic and you're a 100 percent speller, you don't know anything until you know this woman. Mind you, she may not have the exact outside proportions of the one on this picture, but inside they are all the same."

He picked the photograph up, fondled it, and slid it back into the little leather book as he continued. "I'll tell you something. What you've just seen is what life is all about. That woman is made by God just to make you guys into real men. And it isn't something that's bad, it's better than going to Sunday School and getting good marks at school and getting your chores done on time all put together. You haven't begun to learn anything until you've met this woman. Now, I'll tell you how it all works."

He sat back supported on his arms with his hands dug into the moist green grass, his legs stretched straight out ahead of him. "How do you guys feel right now?" It was like a question shot out as a trial balloon by the leader in an adult unstructured lab group in interpersonal relations. How do you cope with that direct kind of feeling question just when you wish you could sink out of the group and do a little hard reflecting on your own. How did I feel? How are you supposed to feel after you've seen your first real hard pornography? I felt good all over and at the same time felt as guilty as if I'd taken the photograph personally. What if down that dusty road right now mom and dad came in the old chev'y looking for me? What if they came and asked what we were doing? I'd feel worse than I did the time mom caught me in the bushes behind the house mixing up fresh eggs from the chicken coop with cream from the milk shed and dried leaves to see what the mixture would look like. I guess the other guys were wondering about this strange mixture of feelings too, because we all looked kind of scared and yet nobody made any motions about getting on home. We wanted to run and we wanted to stay.

"I guess I feel I want to know what you mean by they're all the same inside", mumbled one of the guys. "Yeah, we want to know", we all echoed. Corny's handsome face grinned in a helpful manner as if he understood what we were going through. Maybe he'd felt like this once when he was a kid. "Listen kids, it's one of those things that's hard to understand until you actually get old enough to want to know more about it. But if I show you a bit more you'll one day thank me for letting

SEX EDUCATION OR PORNOGRAPHY

you know this much ahead of time."

He then sat up straight and opened the black book again. With his thumb he nudged out another picture. This one looked more familiar. It was a naked man. We'd all seen our older brothers or our father like this. Except the male organ was very long. It pointed straight up like ours did sometimes in bed or when we took a bath. It was much too long to be believable and we laughed a little as we referred to this incredulity. "It can't be real," one of us commented.

"That's the way it'll be for you," Corny said, "when you see her like she is in this other picture." He held that one up again. "You see, this is Jerry and she's his Jill. When they go up the hill for water sometime and feel like getting together, this is the way it happens. Both feel real good. And when Jill takes all her clothes off it means that Jerry here has to put that long business prong of his right into Jill's nice warm body here," he pointed to the base of her hairline where the legs parted.

"You mean, not from behind like the bulls and cows or the stallions and mares?" asked one of us. "Yeah, really like them, behind sometimes and in front sometimes, except for people it's not just a case of mating-up so's you can have a calf or a colt. Sometimes that's what it's for, but most of the time it's for fun and enjoyment. Let me show you what I mean." He pulled out three more pictures from his book. We gasped at what we saw. The man and woman were interwoven in three different positions on the ground; and I mean the ground. The pictures must have been taken outdoors on a day as hot as this one. One had the man on top; one was the reverse of this position and the other showed the couple lying close to each other in opposite directions, so that their heads were at each others' feet and they were touching each other all over. Again the silence weighed heavily. We had seen more than our adolescent minds and bodies could absorb and sort out. We were in a state of ambivalent disbelief. We knew we could trust Corny but we saw him now as a representative of a strange new world, one which we knew we'd all face one day.

Corny's escapades with the women in the district were well-known. Now we understood why our parents and other adults said they hoped he'd get married to someone who would be strong enough to settle him down. I guess every community has to have people like Corny to be honest about the subject of sex as long as we think we can make it stay in its rightful place through the imposition of censorship laws, and the hiring of more policemen all crying "Permissiveness! It's the ruination of our society!"

Not understanding very many of the implications of this moral situation, we said goodby to Corny and returned to our homes, wiser but not really happier boys.

SEX EDUCATION OR PORNOGRAPHY

To this very day I can't honestly get on the bandwagon with pulpit-thumping moralists who want to rid our towns and cities of printed materials making some allusion to pornography or obscenity. We could triple our police forces and give them open season licenses to shoot on sight any vendor placing magazines containing nude photographs on his newstand but protected kids like me would still get their exposure to the Cornys' society. Without sex education and an understanding of our sexual hangups all the gendarmes in the world cannot enforce standards of morality.

PASTOR'S PUNCH

I always had a certain awesome respect for clergymen. I couldn't equate them to the same classification of humanity, for instance, as railroad conductors, postmen, farmers, doctors, dentists or garbage collectors. With these people I felt pretty much at ease. But I was afraid of clergymen even after being reminded that a minister was a friend of people, including little children. It's like when you know something in your head, intellectually, because your mother told it to you and you believe it, but you feel contrariwise about it in your bones. My mother and father had the greatest respect and love for our clergy, but I just couldn't think of them as real flesh and blood people. To me they were kind of a mixture between a teacher and policeman. I also knew these to be friends, but somehow couldn't believe it.

The United Church minister from Melville customarily made his annual call to our home in the summer somewhere around haying time. It always seemed to happen about a half an hour before dinnertime when my older brother and I were doing something like tramping the hay which Dad and my oldest brother were pitching up into a stack. Our bare feet filled with the morning's quota of thistles would be about at the bursting point when one of us spotted the preacher's car turning in at the gate. Then I'd get all goose pimply and kind of scared inside. Dad would announce that we'd knock off early and get cleaned up for dinner. If the preacher was an ordinary man why did we always have to interrupt something as important as haying to get cleaned up to visit him? And why did all my brothers and sisters suddenly start treating me like something special and calling me by my correct name in front of the minister when I'd be treated my normal abused self in all other situations? It must have been because there was some kind of devious chicanery employed to mask me from some horrible reality. The preacher seemed so tame and harmless; conversation was about nice subjects and said good things about respectable people; everybody behaved so well. Nobody started eating, for example, until mom asked him to say a little prayer, then we all knew no-one helped himself until he was invited to do so. Of course there was the usual devilry taking place under the table that kept the dining room in a semblance of reality. Older brothers and sisters had ways of kicking and punching and pinching designed to cause twitches and squirms without actually fomenting a fight. The fight usually took place later in the unhindered freedom of the back yard when getting even went on in its vicious circle from one day to the next. And there was the explosively dangerous practice of suppressing giggles that moved back and forth from one of us to the next. Someone always pushed the laughter so far down that it erupted out of the rear end with a gurgling gush of wind. All of these things combined to make these little unreal interludes a bit more savory.

Our family was one of only three United Church families around Banner Hall. Most of my friends were Roman Catholic or Lutheran. Our family was in a minority of WASPish background. A lot of the kids spoke Polish or Hungarian or Ukrainian or German in their homes. Often we'd get completely isolated when attempting to rubber in on conversations on the party line because our neighbors would switch to one of these other tongues. It was a good learning experience in empathizing with persons who are alienated by cultural barriers and who are discriminated against when they're outnumbered. I recall one time being so flabbergasted by this form of discrimination on the party line that I used the only Hungarian words I'd ever learned by blurting loudly into the mouthpiece of our phone the Hungarian equivalent of "You go and kiss the dog's ass," to two astonished and momentarily speechless neighbors of that national extraction.

Anyway, getting back to preachers, it was a real treat to be taken by my folks to a service in the rural Lutheran church near Banner Hall. The grandfather of one of my friends had as, they said, passed away and went to heaven. The funeral would be attended by everyone in the community. This would be my first opportunity to see and hear another variety of this strange species referred to as clergymen.

Cars had filled the little churchyard when we arrived. We parked ours outside the fence near the ditch of the road allowance and walked up the hill on top of which stood the immaculately painted white church with the steeple that was a landmark for miles around. We crowded into the back pew; people arriving after us would have to stand behind us. I noticed the beautiful interplay of reflections caused by the sun's rays broken into its component parts as it shone through the stained glass windows. Sparkles and gems played with and chased each other across the glass candle chandelier that hung midway between us and the chancel at the back of which was a large cross. To the left of the cross was a very high pulpit which extended upwards from a deck of steps semi-circling it. There was a small door into the pulpit itself so that when the pastor entered he was boxed in well above his congregation. It was here I received my first impression of the Lutheran minister from Melville, Pastor Birch, whose path would cross mine together with my friends a couple of memorable times again.

Pastor Birch's countenance and dress certainly gave the appearance he was about to say something that had never been divulged before. His glances to the ceiling above the glass chandelier and his other-worldly voice gave the impression he was receiving a message from above of extreme importance which he passed to his listeners below. The translation of this message was undoubtedly aided by his pulpit garb made up of white and scarlet and black material. On this particular instance he couldn't be the same as us; he must be somewhere between where we sat and the voice of God above him. His garments, his voice and the pulpit certainly combined to produce this impression. After a few strange-sounding introductory words by the preacher and a hymn more or less sung in the slowest, draggiest and most unenthusiastic manner by the congregation, I received my first lesson in eschatology.

"Our dear departed friend is not dead; he is only asleep," he began in a deep, sonorous voice. He was a handsome fellow, probably in his thirties. He was quite tall and slim and his dark hair was well groomed and presented his face in good contrast to his colored robes. "Death has no victory over the good shepherd's own lambs. Our friend though old in years is young in God's eternity. The blood of Jesus has been poured out for all of us so that the devil cannot claim us if we receive Him. Such was the case of our dearly beloved neighbor. He accepted Jesus as his savior. He is now with Jesus in glorious surroundings too wonderful for those of us who remain behind to understand." With this reference to a land that had no political boundaries beyond the comprehension of human beings he opened the huge Bible on the pulpit and began to tell us what heaven was really like!

"There will be no weeping; there will be no sadness, only light and rejoicing. Everybody will be friends and there will be no cause for pain or sorrow. The rooms will be in the Lamb's palaces and everything will be in dazzling white and gold; rest and peace will be his forever and ever. It'll be for our friend like sleeping on beds soft like marshmallows comforted by waiting angels playing softly on great harps. Do not weep for him; weep rather for those who are here yet, some in this very room who will not go this way because they have not yet accepted our precious Lord Jesus as their personal saviour." He went on to describe the other place where God would hand over those who made a bad choice where there would be torture by fire and loud weeping and gnashing of teeth. It was a horrible experience, and it had authenticity because the preacher was above us there in that room, getting his inspiration from above that chandelier and some of his words from that massive black book. And his voice rumbled at times like the fearsome clash of thunder preceding an imminent summer storm. How surprising it was then to hear the soft and gentle tones of the same man when he spoke kindly to those crowded around him outside when the commital service was over.

It was at the annual plowing competition that I stood in awe of this man again. The local farmers set aside a day in the summer to show off their latest equipment or their skill at operating older plows as they turned over a new furrow in some volunteer's stubble field or pasture. It was an opportunity to bring your family to view some of the show equipment the machinery dealers in Melville and Yorkton had to offer as well as enter into some good-natured banter over whether horse-drawn equipment did a steadier and more consistent job than some of the new tractor jobs. It was a fun-filled day for kids because we could run in and out around the clustered groups of talking farmers and their visiting wives. We could get as dirty as we wanted to because our mothers knew there was no way in this situation to keep the dust and grime out of our hair and clothes. It was truly a kids' paradise.

Pastor Birch must have thought this would be a good place to get to know his parishioners better because he was here in his white shirt, black tie and suit, moving in and about the groups of farmers. Or maybe it was because the Banner Young Peoples' group associated with his church out here were manning the concession connected with this event. That was quite a laugh in itself for us kids, I mean the title Young Peoples' group. You see it was made up of old men and women in their forties and fifties. It's likely it was started as a young peoples' group twenty or more years ago and although the members grew old the group never disbanded or changed its name. People in groups like this are always telling the rest of us that youth is not a time of life but a state of mind.

Pastor Birch certainly seemed to have no trouble identifying with his parishioners. He may have been their spiritual father image due to the direct channel to God that was evident when he conducted a service but he was more like a friendly neighbour or close relative out here. Except for the fact that he wore such elegant clothing in contrast to the overalls of the farmers he could almost have passed for anyone else. For a clergyman I thought that wasn't too bad.

The chap from the John Deere dealership in Melville announced that the plowing match was to get started. "There will be a contest between the two Massey's, the Case and the John Deere. They will run off together. Following this match we'll stop-watch the two outfits of horses against the four tractor teams." The contestants mounted the big metal horses and filled the air with bursts of back-firing motors and dark grey smoke as they revved their motors and moved the machine-driven plows to the starting line.

My friend Albert dashed up beside me and stage-whispered, "What's the priest doing with all the money?" Albert was Roman Catholic so I could forgive him dubbing Pastor Birch priest. Although you'd wonder why a clever kid like Albert couldn't associate the fact that this preacher was married and had four kids with his misnomer. "What do you mean, money?" I said, without correcting him. "Honest to God, he's been running around behind the cars collecting money from some of those guys back there," he pointed in the direction of the parked cars located not far from the Banner Young Peoples' concession booth. True enough there were maybe a dozen men semi-clustered and Pastor Birch was just taking a bill from one of them. "Let's move over and see," I offered.

The tractors were now puffing up enthusiasm and self-confidence for the take-off and it was difficult to hear the conversation, but before the pistol was fired to signal the start we caught Pastor Birch's words, "Okay, fellows, remember, I'm the banker. Two of us on the John Deere, five on the first Massey and two each on the Case and the other Massey. Winners split fairly. The banker takes 10 percent!" Crack! sounded the pistol, the group dispersed and followed the rest of the crowd, men waving their arms, women forgetting their station in life and cheering madly and kids shoving each other to be the first to get their bare feet in the furrows of the freshly plowed sod. It felt so good that us kids almost forgot what the whole affair was about. The end of the race came too soon.

The dealer from Melville waved his arms in a fan like motion and the drivers shut down their machines and jumped to the ground. "The winner is Johnny Gadeigza with his John Deere special!" he proudly announced, "far be it for me to say anything more. But just look at that green beauty," he teased.

I don't think pastor Birch wanted anybody else to notice the roll of bills he'd collected because he'd shoved them into this suit coat pocket and was now shaking the hands of the contestants and being a really great guy with all the people. The plaudits completed, the crowd dispersed to re-assemble in smaller groups amongst which was the pastor's budding gamblers. It was to these men he returned. Albert and I noticed that he retrieved the roll of bills from his pocket and with the expertise of a veteran bank teller slivered off several of them to each of the two men who had obviously taken odds on the John Deere's success. He pocketed a handful of remaining greenbacks. The intermediary between God and man in the pulpit at the top of the little spiral staircase was the beneficiary between man and man in the field. Perhaps he was a literalist, "Render unto God the things that are God's and unto Caesar, the things that are Caesar's." Certainly he was a man who enjoyed and played at the games people play. He had other human qualities, too.

Sunday afternoons during June and July were used mostly for the Sunday picnics. In later years we called them sportsdays. Each school district and community organization sponsored its own. Banner Hall community was no exception; in fact, because of its relatively massive facilities, a large ground area allowing two softball fields, not including the one in the adjacent Runneberg schoolyard, ample racing area for the variety of footraces, and the hall itself against which the booth or poplar branch-covered concession could be built, accommodated all the ingredients for a really successful picnic. If the weather co-operated, large crowds came from near and far to cheer for their own ball team and to engage in the fun and competition of a number of activities. We kids mostly enjoyed hanging around the booth looking for lost coins for which we traded hot dogs and over-sized country-style ice cream cones. Also, if you hung around long enough an elderly neighbor or an uncle or somebody might feel a surge of compassion and buy a hungry-looking kid a treat. It usually worked one way or another.

On one such hot Sunday afternoon the Banner Hall picnic was well underway. Albert and I had been observing the truckloads of brightly clad ball players from Melville, Fenwood, Birmingham, Duff, Willowbrook and several other villages disembark and sort out their equipment. We wandered over to the racing area and heard one of the officials give a rundown on the forthcoming three-legged, relay and potato bag races. We particularly wanted to be around for the latter because it was always a huge source of fun to see our moms, dads, teachers and other authoritative figures make fools of themselves falling all over the grounds as they attempted to jump and hop twenty yards in a burlap sack in the hopes of being the first to cross the chalked finish line. Having satisfied ourselves of the approximate chronological order of these athletic contests we swaggered over to the side of the bush separating the large ball diamond from the north end of Banner Hall and the concession booth. If there was anything mysterious going on it was usually happening in this vicinity.

We noticed that Pastor Birch's shiny black Buick had arrived. His car was always shiny. I remember how on the day of the plowing match, some of us kids has sat up on the front fenders of this beauty and one of the officials chased us off giving us the devil for daring to get dust on the black metal. Today there were no traces of the grimy smudges left by our overalls nor were there the mudstains usually seen on other automobiles after their nose dives through the variety of potholes on the dirt roads between Banner Hall and Melville. Pastor Birch must have been a very careful driver and he obviously exercised great care in grooming his belongings.

The car was parked with the trunk half hidden under the soft branches of several young poplars. We assumed that it was being protected from the hot sun and still offered a front seat view of the ball games which were now underway in the diamond just ahead. But a crowd had gathered along the third to home base line and any spectator sitting in the car would not be able to view the proceedings. Albert and I decided that there must be another reason for this car being backed into the bush and we resolved to hang around and see what this unpredictable man might be up to. "Maybe he's going to accept bets on the teams," I said. Albert conjectured that he'd make money faster if he was to do it on the races. Anyway, we'd wait and see. We'd just fix ourselves like a couple of monkeys looping our fingers through the chicken-wire backstop behind the catcher and digging our toes into the soft grass at its base and jiggling back and forth whenever a hit was made or a good catch retrieved in the outfield. Pastor Birch was moving back and forth amongst the lines of rooters and fans on both sides of the softball diamond.

He was easy to spot and follow. Again he wore a black suit and white shirt and tie. Being Sunday we figured he came directly to the picnic from the service in Melville or from the little Lutheran church not far from Banner Hall. Almost everybody else was casually dressed and nobody else wore a jacket. But in keeping with a minister's role I suppose he was expected to be more uncomfortable than anyone else. His clothing, however, didn't impede his activity. When he wasn't extolling with a cheer some player who had executed a skillful maneuver, he was engaging in what appeared to be earnest counselling with one of his male parishioners. He moved in this way from one end of the crowd to the other being careful not to offend any of the men by excluding him from his personal greeting and if the occasion seemed right, a more involved conversation.

The score was now tied up. The crowd had polarized neatly into two camps of supporting fans. Sunday softball fever had reached its highest point. Attention was glued on two people, the pitcher and the batter. Encouraging cries like "Go get it tiger! Hit it into the wheat field!" and counter cries like, "Aw, go home to mother! You can't hit the broadside of a barn door!" were heard. And for the pitcher "Come on, fella, take your time, you've got his number!" was offset with "Lookit the pitcher! He's running scared! He's paralyzed, he can't let go of the ball!" Nobody was looking anywhere else right now. Nobody, that is, except Pastor Birch and a half dozen of the men he'd been talking to.

"For cryin' out loud, lookit that!" exclaimed Albert as he let go of the screen we'd set into a nice swaying motion with our excitement. I joined him and faced the direction of his pointing finger. "Well, I'll be tatooed all over," I responded using words I heard a guy in a sailor suit say one night at a dance. "Where in heck are they going? And at a time like this, it doesn't make sense." Pastor Birch and his friends were walking briskly towards his car. They seemed to want to get away while everyone else was glued to the spectator's drama on the softball diamond. They didn't get into the car, rather they walked right past it and entered the bush on one side of the trunk. They had to grab the branches and make an opening for themselves because at this time of the year the trees were luxuriantly wrapped in the biggest leaves. The army worms or the drought would get to them later.

Grade eight boys' curiosity and questions about what adults do when they look as if they're hiding from somebody had a greater power of persuasion than observing the outcome of a power squeeze at a spectator sport. We were off like a couple of jack rabbits. "Let's go this way," Albert whispered as we wheeled around the corner of the bush so as to keep out of sight of the men and enter the woods near the hall. We knew where all the little winding paths went because we'd made a lot of them ourselves in our cowboys and Indian games played at recess. We had the advantage of a couple of highly trained spies who could literally duck through the bushes without cracking a branch. We'd sneak up from behind and see what Pastor Birch had going with these guys.

Loud cheers went up from the softball field. It sounded as if the batter had connected because cries of "Go! Go! Go! Don't look back. You're in for a homer!" shrieked through the bush. Albert and I made good time under the barrage of shouts and boos. We crouched behind a couple of bent, old poplars and shielded by a spattering of greens and browns we observed Pastor Birch and his buddies standing in the bushes that shaded the back end of his Buick from the direct sun. He was stooped over facing the trunk lid; as the cries of the softball fans died down we heard the click of a key in the trunk lock and observed the contents of a well stocked compartment as the clergyman forced the trunk lid into the weight of the dewy soft branches. In the trunk of that black unscratched beauty was an array of shiny whiskey and beer bottles like we'd seen in the back of a mountie's car one night at a dance when he'd arrested a man for bootlegging and confiscated his stock. "Holy cow!" Albert muttered, "Let's get out of here before we get caught." "We're not doing anything wrong," I pleaded in a whisper for Albert to wait. "If they see us we'll tell'em we're just having a pee, or something." We crouched down so that the bare knees below our short pants pressed into the moist leaf mold of the underbrush.

Pastor Birch now whispered gleefully in a kind of come and get it voice, "What'll you have?" and reached in to select whatever it was each man requested. The bottles made only a faint click as they were handled. Some beer bottles were opened and emptied on the spot. One almost hit us as it was flung empty into the depths of the bush. Some larger flask type bottles were unscrewed, passed around and then replaced carefully in their cases. A certain amount of unmanlike giggling and militia-like comments such as "Praise the Lord and pass the ammunition," rose in the shrouded secrecy of this little group of Lord's Day celebrators. Now the men were reaching into their pockets and peeling off bills while the pastor made change again with the expertise of the cashier in Athey's grocery store in Melville. The trunk lid was closed just as quietly as it had been opened. The men waited out the relative hush of the softball game. Another excited cry went up and our vigil came to an end with the rapid departure of the minister and his friends as they melted into the cheering throngs of enthusiastically shouting fans. Their absence would not be noted, but their breath was a little stronger the next time they added their voices to support a nervous batter or a tiring pitcher.

Our community observed rigidly enforced liquor laws. In the minds of Grade sixers alcohol and good citizenship never mixed. Most of us grew up conditioned to believe that drinking was not only harmful it was sinful. We knew it went on whenever people gathered to have fun and enjoy themselves, but we also knew that our lips would never taste such demon-filled liquid. I guess we would be a new breed of citizenry, thinking right thoughts and obediently observing the taboos of our culture. Pastor Birch and other pioneers of the human spirit helped erase the notion that utopias are built by the suppression of human needs. For every rigid law enforcer there's a guardian of human dignity who will discover a subtle means or a crude loophole to expose man's real humanity.

WHEN I SHOT THE DOG

The day I shot our neighbor's straying dog left an indelible wound on my spirit.

Except for our farm dog I've not been a dog fancier. But when I look into a dog's eyes I feel guilty. Somehow I get the feeling that the mongrel or the pooch or the high breed is reminding me of the wicked deed visited upon his relative of many years ago.

Every farm boy has good memories of some dog in his life. They've been more than pets. Dogs are the unlikely receivers of childhood confidences and they don't betray these. They're pals of the deepest order. They can reflect feelings of joy and pain and are capable of quietly assimilating the moods of their masters. They're intensely sensitive creatures whose feelings register in their eyes, the quiver of their ears and the flick of their tail.

The dog of my early childhood was named "Jet". Of course he was black as coal. He had long gangly legs and a slim, wiry body that evolved into a strong masculine neck. His head epitomized perkiness and shrewdness. His eyes registered the required mood whether of gentleness, nervousness, playfulness or anger. I looked upon Jet as my companion, confidant, adviser and protector. That last role is not an uncommon one for a small boy's dog to fulfill. I recall, for example, when mother was in the hospital for several days when my young brother was born. My father, brothers and sisters seemed always to be out of the house when I needed them most. Jet was my protector against the demons and wild animals that seemed ready to pounce at me from every mysterious crackle and knock in the walls.

Still being of the impressionable age of a first grader, I believed that monsters of almost unimaginable dimensions lurked behind every unopened door and were ready to leap at me from every shadowy corner of the house. Jet seemed to comprehend my fear and sympathize with my weakness. There was an unarticulated compact between us that was deep and tender.

On one morning when everyone else had gone from the house, the moans and scratches produced by the winds blowing through the poplar and Saskatoon berry bushes against the back of the house, coupled with the usual cracking sounds that originated upstairs and down in the basement, yielded images in my mind of villains approaching from several directions about to descend upon me for the kill. I pushed the old round kitchen table against the wall and surrounded it with wooden chairs so that the legs interlocked in sentry fashion. Leaving only an opening beside the wall I enticed Jet into the little wooden cell formed under the table top by crawling ahead of him with a bone. When we had settled in, I placed my arms around his strong neck and rolled over with his taut body at my side. There for the next two or three hours we waited. I still felt scared but a bit more secure from the unknown invaders. Only dogs and little boys really understand such things. And these are the kind of affections that tear one's heart strings when in later years, like in Grade 8, you betray such trust.

"Kilback's dog should be shot!" Dad exclaimed on several occasions. "She runs wild and they don't do a thing to keep the bitch at home" On this particular occasion, a bitterly cold but still and sunny January Sunday, Dad said to me, "If you want to put that poor beast out of its misery, go ahead." The dog was skulking up from a bush towards the barn. It was about two hours prior to sunset and the ice crystals were descending, reflecting chains of jewels. The animal cast a long shadow across the pearly snow as she approached the steaming barn door. She was hungry again and would momentarily be causing a commotion amongst the chickens and the cattle in her frantic attempt to find something to eat.

I was always relatively quick to respond to a request or an order from my parents. Obedience in those days was expected and it was easier to fall in line than it was to enter into a dialogue or discussion about the merits or philosophy behind a certain act. And to honor this kind of request meant the opportunity to adventure into an experience never tried before. Besides I was always willing to test out a suggestion even if the order hadn't actually been given. On one such occasion Mother had been jokingly, I learned to my chagrin later, expounding to a neighbor in the kitchen on the irreplaceable value of a certain large brown milk jug. "I don't know how many times I've dropped this thing," she laughed, "but it simply will not be broken. It can't be broken; I've even dropped in on the cement in the basement and it wouldn't break. Such a remarkable jug!"

That was all the encouragement and challenge I needed. When Mom had turned her and the neighbor's attention to a new hooked rug she had hooked, I surreptitiously slipped over to the cupboard to take a closer look at the earthenware container that for years held the family milk supply at every meal. The jug was about half-filled. I looked closely at the detail along the rim and along the outside.

There were a few little niches and cracks in it that made it appear a little less than unbreakable. However it may be that way just because it's very old, I thought. I'd give it a real test.

Outside the old cow barn the cat dishes were arranged on a small pile of flattish rocks to allow for the feeding of a large number of the feline species necessary to keep rats and mice away from the bars and feed bins. This would be a good place to test my mother's shatter-proof vessel. I dumped the milk into the dishes. Extending the jug high above my head at arms' length, I snapped my arms down and let the jug crash broadside against a rock. The results were indeed gratifying. The jug, in fact, was not a miracle product. Picking up a few of the splintered remains I dashed back to the house. Kicking open the kitchen door I proudly announced, "Hey Mom! You know that old milk jug you've been trying for years to break? Look what I've done! It was simple!"

Sometimes it's easier to follow a suggestion that was never really intended than it is to carry out a direct order. Maybe the suggestion that I shoot the neighbor's dog was not so much a directive as it was an opportunity for me to test out my own curiosity and cruelty quotient.

I had used a .22 rifle for a couple of years. Indeed I was considered by my parents to be a fairly good shot. Prairie chickens and ducks were often the unsuspecting victims of some of my Sunday afternoon excursions when after literally slithering along the ground on my belly, pushed along by my legs and pulled by the free hand that didn't carry the rifle, I crawled through stubble or grass to a slough's edge or beside a flock of chickens feeding in the field and took aim at a single bird. It was only in the last summer that I had tried the shotgun.

Albert and I smuggled the family shotgun out of its holder in the back porch one day after school. He had four or five twelve guage shells that he had pilfered out of his older brother's supply. We decided to try this new venture in a team effort even to the point of aiming the gun and pulling the trigger. Just north of the house beyond the bush was the dugout; behind the dugout and beside the road allowance was the hill or mound formed by the clay out of this manmade water hole. This offered good cover for anyone wanting to sneak up on a flock of ducks which happened to be frolicking on the dugout. There were almost always some birds there. We crawled along the ditch beside the road until we got behind the yellow grey mound. While Albert crouched at the base, in reptile fashion I glided up the side of the clay pile until with one eye over a rock I appraised the waterfowl situation on the surface of the dugout. There were five of them. Two greenheads and three mallard hens. Real beauties. And they weren't in any way aware of intruders and impending doom. They were clustered near the edge of the water in what I considered was an ideal shotgun pattern. Albert and I had studied commercial pictures of the manner in which shot pellets held together in a choked pattern for maybe twenty yards and then spread out to encompass the game. From short range we knew you could blow a large hole right through a rabbit. From this range it would be possible to hit all five birds. I slid back into the ditch and told Albert.

It was a matter that required considerable care. Neither of us had ever fired a shotgun before. Our gun was an old double-barreled veteran with an intricately engraved stalk. We put two of Albert's five shells in the chambers and very cautiously pushed the gun ahead of us up the embankment behind the rock from which I had surveyed the prey. With both of us flat on our tummies we slid the barrels over the rock. Hearts pounding we each pulled back and cocked a hammer. While I aimed the weapon at the unsuspecting ducks and pushed back with both arms completely extended holding onto the butt of the gun, Albert reached forward to pull the rear trigger. When the tip of the barrels seemed to be in line with my right eye and the ducks I said "Now!" and Albert squeezed the trigger. What a calamity! Both barrels discharged simultaneously and I ducked as the gun whizzed over my head and down the bank. The ducks, all five of those beauties, quacked derisively as they took off together for another pond. We learned that a gun, especially a shotgun, must be held firmly against one's shoulder before it is fired. The kick would not be as great. A few subsequent lessons with dad insured safety in the presence of shotguns. Now I was prepared to shoot a dog and I would use that same shotgun as the weapon.

It is a myth that little children are naive and innocent until smudged by the evil example of their elders. It is true that each person has great capacity for evil and for good. Through practice, trial and error and experimentation we learn how to deal with the potential powers and forces that strain to be unleashed within us. Once we become free enough and independent enough to choose the kinds and styles of powers we would unleash then we decide what we shall become and how we will interact with the fellows and creatures and nature around us.

When I decided I would interpret Dad's suggestion to mean that I should kill the dog I chose that action not from the force of external obedience but from the motivation of an internal urge to wage war on another being. It's almost a neat trick to dub the enemy in a war an animal-like name. The Americans used the name "gook" instead of Vietnamese and made the killing of Communists a kind of game between human and less than human. we used the term "redskin" when exploiting our Indian neighbor and thus labelled these dignified beings something akin to animal hides. Japs, Dagos, Nazis, Ukes all have their unfortunate demise using this psychological treat. But if we look deeply at one human or one animal we cannot get away with this. The laws of creation and survival catch up to us and betray our wicked intentions. I guess maybe that's why we avoid looking into each other's eyes.

The object of my pent-up rage and cruelty happened to be a relatively defenceless creature. One could not even call the bitch the prey or the hunted because the animal had already lost its sense of dignity, its ownership and its source of livelihood. I would use this animal like all boys in Grade 8 use animals or wounded people; like all men exploit the handicapped, not the physically, but the economically hurt and the underprivileged, to vent their rage, their cruelty and their need to dominate. And I would do it in the name of duty just as all men do it in the name of justice or business or survival.

The dog had run out of the barn door as if sensing trouble. She ran through the bush south of the barn and I thought I was going to lose sight of her. A feeling of disappointed panic began to surge through me. I knew I wanted to kill that animal and I didn't want her to outwit me. I ran to the house for the shotgun and loaded it with a number 2. Experience had taught me that if I could fire within a few yards the shot would result in sudden death. But where did that animal go?

I ran through the snow hoping to get ahead of the dog if perchance she stopped in the bushes. By circling the bluff I would head her back into the yard if that was the case. The snow was unmarked at the far side of the trees; no animal or person had crossed from there to the open field beyond. She must still be in there. I'd start into the bush and shoot her. It was getting exciting, my heart began to thump and my mouth went dry. Would she suddenly realize what was up and turn on me? The idea had a certain appeal. I might be involved in a life and death battle between man and vicious beast. She might spring towards me and fasten her long teeth from her protruding bony jaw into my wrist shaking the gun out of my hand; then she would pull me into the snow and tear into my throat severing my jugular vein. I must be vigilant and watchful and listen for any sound which would betray the animal's hiding place. I would stalk this unholy beast and become a hero for my skill and care.

The bushes ahead of me thickened as I moved toward the centre of the bluff. Like many prairie bluffs this was poplar-circled with a receding core which in the summer was potholed and waterlogged. Around the old buffalo wallows near the middle grew scraggly willow bushes bunched out from central rooting systems. These intertwined at the top where the bushes locked into each other's branches. In order to traverse the bush centres a person had to crouch down and push the branches apart. I was now in this position, wading knee deep in fluffy snow expecting to confront my foe the next time I pulled back a branch.

The dog had entered this area directly opposite me. Her keen ears, of course, had made a mockery of my best woodsmanship. She knew exactly where I was as I stealthily approached her. But rather than retreat, she waited behind one of the large black willow clusters hoping that I'd miss her. I saw the tracks she had made as she bounded through the snow; they approached my direction and appeared to go one way only. I knew she must be within a few feet of where I stood and listened for a crackling branch or an animal's breathing. I tried to suppress my own loud breathing and the pounding in my ears, but as I concentrated both seemed to get louder. I cocked the shotgun and moved forward very carefully.

I caught sight of the end of a larger depression in the snow behind the next clump of willows as I cautiously proceeded. This would be where she was crouching. She would be bundled tight almost in a ball near the base of the tree. I got down on my knees and inched ahead on my forelegs letting them act like snowshoes pressing against my overalls. The moment of violent action was imminent. Would I be able to keep my pounding pulse and perspiring body under control? Now I could see the rear end of the animal brown against the snow even as I spotted it quivering as the dog pulled her body into a tighter ball. "Kill the beast!" I thought to myself. "The dirty thieving bitch has the nerve to try and hide from me, putting me through this ordeal. Kill the bitch and let her blood spray red streaks on the white snow like a chicken when its head is severed by the farmer's axe.

I stood upright and pulled the shotgun up to my shoulder, aiming it at that portion of the dog visible to me. Then I took a step forward and with a villainous cry, "Die you bastard!" I squeezed the trigger. Half of the poor dog's right rear thigh exploded and splattered a weird pattern of hair, flesh, bone and blood on the ivory surface of that erstwhile serene patch of snow. The dog gave a pain-filled shriek and made a complete flip in the air turning to face me with front paws extended. "My God what have I done?" I moaned as those eyes met mine and eradicated any man-beast barriers that existed a few seconds earlier. I was now looking eye ball to eye ball at another being and I couldn't cope with all the feelings of that confrontation. "Poor doggie, don't die; don't hurt. I didn't mean to hurt you," I began to stammer. I reached out a fearful hand that begged for some kind of miracle that would change everything and make the scene beautiful again. How I would like to be rolling in the snow with this pooch making believe we were rescuing each other from drowning or suffocating or something. Those wishful flashes however could not be. I had wounded to kill and she was bleeding to death. I wished I didn't have to look at that well-shaped head and those entreating eyes that were saying, "How could you do it? You the friend of little animals; you whom dogs have loved and protected. Others I could suspect, but why you?" A member of God's created order was suffering. I caused it and I must act again. I began to chafe under the growing-up that was taking place there in the snow. "I have to put that poor defenceless animal out of its misery," I thought and began to reload the gun. This was the beginning of a torture that involved me and the dog for the next two hours.

With hope running out the dog made one last desperate attempt at survival. With only three quarters of her body at her command and that lacking the blood and energy required for strength, she pulled herself forward with her fore legs and pushed her remaining shattered rear out of the hole in the snow with her one good back leg and turned away from me in retreat. In a few seconds she was out of sight behind the willows where the atrocity took place. I couldn't believe it. I fumbled the shell in my hand and missed getting it in the chamber letting it drop out of view into the deep snow. I set the gun against the tree and kicked the snow in a vain attempt to find the shell. Seconds were wasting and the animal was suffering. What had gone wrong with my coordination and hunting skill? I was desperate. Why did I waste time looking for a dropped bullet when I had another in my pocket? I sprang forward re-loading the gun as I moved.

The fresh blood trail taunted me as I pursued the wounded whining dog! I pushed my way pell mell through the wild shrubs letting the willow branches strike my face in the cold. I wanted, I needed to suffer. Let the twigs spear my eyes, let the icy cold freeze my face, let the branches scourge my neck and cut my ears. "Doggie don't run!" I pleaded as I lost time in the snow. How could she move so fast?

When I got to the outer rim of poplar trees I saw to my utter amazement and adding to my desperate anxiety the wounded animal was heading south away from our farm and apparently picking up speed and strength as she mobilized what was left of her to fulfill her last mission in life. How it was possible at all, I leave for hunters to explain. Ducks and prairie chickens are known to survive long agonized periods of waiting for slow death when badly wounded in the blast, fall to the ground and escape being picked up immediately. Big game like deer and moose may wander for miles and miles after being filled with the shrapnel of the bursting bullet in their flesh, calling on all their creative resources for life and survival, finally dying painfully in some remote spot considered absolutely inaccessible by the hunter.

The dog was moving away from me at a rate much faster than I could master in that kind of deep snow. I'd have to think of another way. I ran around the bush towards the barn where I bridled a horse and pursued the poor beast on horseback.

By the time I picked up the blood trail again it was getting dark. I feared losing the animal completely. However the horse made much faster time through the snow than either I or the dog could navigate it. I could see the animal ahead in the dusky murkiness of that cold winter evening. She was now almost finished as she pulled her halting body into the side of a snowbank formed by the January winds blowing over some scattered silver willows. There she stretched out and placed her head over her paws and slanted it sideways just a little to helplessly watch me approach. I jumped into the snow and tied my mount to a protruding branch. Filled with remorse and sorrow I approached the offended victim.

Communication involves much, much more than the sharing of words between two human beings. We are aware of that. We communicate love, hatred, suspicion, jealousy, trust and the whole gamut of the emotional spectrum through a glance, a touch, a frown or a smile. Sometimes the silence between us communicates the more authentic sentiments than the words we use to embellish or hide our feelings. We have a great deal to learn about human communication but we are working at it. But we know little about communication amongst animals and especially between the other animals and the human species.

Many quiet summer mornings in pre-school day would find me sitting on a knoll at the entrance of a gopher hole. Here I learned through experience that even those little animals, which were judged wicked by human standards because they ate wheat, had feelings and worked through their thought processes. One particular little gopher I dubbed "Niki" became very trusting in my presence. That was because I sat very still for maybe two hours and let him know that I trusted him, too. A small boy and a gopher could communicate. We learned a little about each other not because I studied him but because like two equal beings we in a strange and almost mystical way got to explore each other in motionless reflection. Now I would enter into a heart-breaking experience with an animal I used to deal with the frustration of acting out my need to be cruel.

In the eyes of that poor wretch now completely debased by my debauchery I could see the philosophical questions of the ages long before I would confront these questions in an intellectual context. The question about existence was there. What's it all for and who are we? What is this thing we call life that can be so wonderful and so debased and to which we cling when threatened with every last ounce of energy? Why do creatures spend their days in a rush of pursuits for food and survival? Why do they hurt each other in the process when you know finally in a moment such as this that we really need each other? Stricken animal and victorious hunter for a few seconds the philosophical treasures of the centuries teased us. But I must now perform an act of love. There comes a place in life where our evil intentions push our actions beyond the point of return. To do nothing then is to accept the coward's last resort. To act is to close the chapter on a bad irretrievable experience that will never again be encouraged. I raised the gun, cocked the hammer and blew that poor animal's head to shreds. Then I wept.

UP THE ELEVATOR SHAFT

My Uncle Bert was the agent of the Wheat Pool elevator at Brewer four miles south of our farm. Albert lived halfway between our place and Brewer so whenever I walked to see my uncle and aunt I dropped in on Albert to coax him to come along. He never needed much encouragement because grain elevators and railroad tracks offered the kind of mystery boys like Albert and I really liked to explore. Also, Uncle Bert was one of the nicest guys between Melville and Yorkton.

I guess elevator agents are a special brand of humanity. They've got to be everything from botanist and students of agronomics to group leaders and marriage counsellors. Not only do they need to know seed varieties, grades and market quotations but they've got to have skills in the whole human relations bag. Hardened farmers have been known to break down in the office of their elevator agent and blurt out personal problems they'd never tell a relative or a priest. There seems to be some therapeutic value in unloading grain in the big grain pit. The association between dumping the hard-earned cash product down the hole and exposing the recesses of the psyche is truly remarkable. Somehow knowing that everything goes into that pit, all the dockage and the good grain together, seems to loosen up the inner tension and compounded frustration in the grain grower's private life. The agent is at hand weighing, grading and quoting prices. He's friendly and open, asking easily about the wife and kids knowing which of the latter has been playing hockey and who has been ill and who'll be home for summer holidays. His neutrality makes him an easy mark for advice. His listening ear is so accessible. In his office over coffee the story is dumped out in the same explosive manner as the grain gushed out the tailgate of the wagon or truck with the lift raised and the locks released.

While playing around in the engine room in the basement of the office, on one occasion I overheard such an encounter. I loved to climb around the two huge flywheels of Uncle Bert's elevator engine. It was one of those old style piston jobs that gave a double "Bang-Bang" as it ran. With a wheezing noise, it jerked into motion when Uncle Bert placed his shoulder against one of the wheels getting it underway.

I was standing with my feet on the lower rim of one of those wheels trying to create that wheezing, coughing sound in the cylinder when I heard a coffee cup bang down on the table above and an exasperated voice say, "I dunno what I'm going to do with her. I just don't know! She's been flying back and forth between the bunkhouse and the house like a magpie flitting from the bush to the chicken feed."

"Tell me a little about it," Uncle Bert responded in his quiet, empathetic way.

"I should be able to settle it myself, I really shouldn't bother you with my problems."

"If it makes you feel better, talk about it," Uncle Bert said encouragingly. leaning back in his wooden cradle chair, I could hear his feet scrape across the floor. I climbed down off the fly wheel and tiptoed over to the foot of the steps pretending to examine labels on some tin pails stacked near the wall in case one of the men should spot me there.

"I don't know what's happening between Alice and me," he said slowly with a deep sigh. "I get so mad when I see what I think is going on that I'm scared sometimes I'm going to do something really stupid." There was a long silence. Uncle Bert wasn't bothered by this kind of non-verbal communication. The man needed time to get hold of himself. He was getting very honest about identifying some really frightening feelings and there was a bit of therapy in that silence. It bothered me though because I couldn't see them and I missed out on the accompanying facial expressions. I was afraid I was going to cough or suddenly have to go to the toilet or something.

"Alice and I haven't been too close now for a couple of years," finally came the follow-up. "I work hard. Maybe I'm working harder because I don't know how else to deal with this," he said sadly. "Like, I do things around the yard at night I didn't use to do. You know, bang away at something in the shop. Check the livestock, anything to keep out of the house until she's in bed, then I come in tired and fall asleep. Then there's Jim." His voice dropped when he said that, as if Jim's name spelled doom.

"You've had him for five years," Uncle Bert observed quietly, "he's been a good man."

"Yeah, that's it. He's my right arm out there. Couldn't operate the whole section without him. Knows more about the purebred shorthorns and registered seed than I do. Keeps the whole place in order like a master gardener. Fixes up the barn and the house like it was his own domain." So Jim was the hired man. Now I knew who was talking to Uncle Bert; they lived just three miles from us.

"You think maybe Jim's been too handy, eh?" said Uncle Bert. "Maybe he's been fixing things around the house a little too much."

"Well, to me it's out of hand. Like I said she's been flitting between the house and the bunkhouse a heck of a lot. And I've never been able to say anything, and I'm scared of doing anything; I feel like such a helpless fool!" He sounded to me to be on the verge of tears. I felt all choky and sort of trapped there in the basement. Again there was a long pause.

People don't appreciate it much but it's a fact that some of the best counselling in this country is done not by doctors, social workers, psychiatrists and ministers but by guys like Uncle Bert. Open, non-gossipy types who really make a man feel like a person. It was happening right above me right now.

The farmer began again haltingly, "Well, when I think about it, you know I could've seen it happening a long time ago but I guess I was afraid to face the thought. Jim and Alice started hitting it off too friendly, if you know what I mean, a couple of years ago. I guess I just made it easier for them. I liked Jim so darned much and trusted him with anything on the farm so I played along. He and Alice used to stay too long over coffee, for example, when I got up from the table to mind the cows. I'd just go out laughing; when I think of it now I sure played dumb. We all seemed to be having such a good time together, the three of us. I should've been on the ball when Alice started to cool towards me in bed about the same time. You know, she'd say 'Not tonight hon, I'm so tired,' and I'd let it go. But it got scarcer and scarcer, if you know what I mean, and she always seemed tired. But I'd started noticing how she'd slip out to Jim's bunkhouse more often than necessary for cleaning and the like and when Jim was in there, too. And I just kept lettin' it happen. Now here I am, big, well-known farmer with all the know-how, all screwed up!" There followed a heck of a long quiet. I started to feel real uneasy.

"You're afraid of saying anything or doing anything as you say because of confirming what you already suspect," summarized Uncle Bert. "You're afraid of what this whole thing is going to do to you. I mean your reputation as a great manager and a good husband. Where is it getting you by letting it go on?"

"I hate to admit, goddamit, but yeah, I'm scared. I guess I think I've lost Alice already and Jim is such a great guy maybe I'm scared I can't manage without him." He sounded so pitiful. What was Uncle Bert going to do now.

"Have some more coffee," he said. I heard the movement of feet and the clink of cups, the pouring sound of liquid.

"Thanks," said the farmer.

Uncle Bert was walking around now, mug in hand. I could imagine him standing with his back to the poor guy, looking out the window and appearing deep and contemplative. He did this a lot. "Supposing you were to go to Alice and really tell her how you feel: I don't mean nastily or in a rough sort of way but kind of the way you are right now; what do you think would happen?"

"I guess she'd be real surprised. In the first place I've never acted hurt like this in front of anybody but you; in the second place, she'd likely be amazed that I know what's going on; but I don't think I could do it," he replied

"Is there something really great, terrifically manly about being able to hold in your feelings?" Uncle Bert raised his gentle voice a little. "Do you think you're a bigger man because you can bash machinery and livestock around but you can't talk about some personal problem between you and Alice. Are you a man?" he seemed to taunt, "Are you?"

"Oh God, cut that out," he jumped to his feet. Another pause in conversation and the sound of shuffling feet. "But then I guess you're right; if I go on like this it'll all end up on the heap anyway. If I get up enough guts to talk about it, at least I'll know and she'll know that I care." More silence "But what if I have to fire Jim and what if Alice goes with him. Oh, Lord, I couldn't face it. But maybe it could still maybe, work somehow."

"Maybe," responded Uncle Bert. After more silence the two men walked out and I was able to slip up the stairs and out of the office before Uncle Bert came back from the elevator. As I said before, I had a lot of respect for Uncle Bert. So did Albert. He's one of the big reasons we like to horse around his elevator. I guess we caused him quite a bit of suffering too.

Although Uncle Bert wasn't a hefty man, the combined weight of Albert and me wouldn't add up to his stature. This is important to remember if you're going to ride up in the one man hoist that grain agents used to get up to the higher floors of their elevator. The hoist is rigged up with pulleys, ropes, some weights and a little platform with a foot break. To go up you released the brake and pulled up on the ropes. The weights were there to balance the man's weight in such a way that he could pull the hoist up and when he wanted to descend all he had to do was push his foot on the brake lever and the platform would lower under the force of gravity. Albert and I were told on various occasions to stay away from the hoist and we were never to climb up the wall ladder to the higher bins. One day we figured we'd give it a try anyway.

Uncle Bert had gone over to the house to have coffee with my aunt. Albert and I

UP THE ELEVATOR SHAFT

walked through the elevator entrance, across the grill over the dump pit, along the dusty floor to the giant wooden hopper into which the grain spilled from the various bins above guided by a myriad of chutes. In this area sparrows chirped and messed all over everything. Dust was thick on the two by fours that stuck out from the walls and was half an inch deep on the floor. Directly beneath the tallest part of the building and against the wall in the dark was the little hoist. We decided to give it a work-out of just a couple of feet.

Whenever the devil tempts young boys to experiment as we were now about to do, he allows you a few strange tingling feelings along the spine which gets you scared for a few seconds. It's done obviously to enhance the operation a bit. If you just go ahead and grab and eat the forbidden fruit without at least having a last minute second thought and a good twinge of conscience, temptation wouldn't add up to much and going against someone's explicit command would have no depth of enjoyment. Albert and I both experienced this twinge or gut lightning about the same time. He looked at me just as I was looking at him. "Do you think we should?" he asked.

"I dunno why we shouldn't," I replied, but wanting really to postpone it or call it off. It's so much easier to disobey when you've got someone else who is as chicken as you are but just nervy enough to be mutually strengthened by the other's boastful words. "We're almost as heavy together as Uncle Bert," I said, "and we're only going to take her up a couple of feet. Heck, even if we can't get her down again, which I know we will, we can lock her there and jump off. Uncle Bert will think he just forgot to bring her all the way down." Such rationalizing wasn't really convincing either of us but it was the kind of token concern we needed to take the plunge. "I'll just run back and see if Uncle Bert is still at the house." I was back in a flash and the two of us clambered on to the platform and grabbed the ropes.

"Release the brake," Albert ordered as the two of us pulled down on the dusty hemp. Up we shot. Boy, it felt good! We shot up about eight feet on the first tug. I took my foot off the lever. We looked around and saw the first deck surrounding a row of bins. It was a dusty, dark world untravelled by most humans. Here we were where only Uncle Bert and some elevator maintenance men had traversed. "Let her go again," I said as I released the brake and we pulled on the ropes, hand over hand, upwards we shot. There is simple joy in disobedience. A charge of exciting energy ran through me and infused me with delightful euphoria. We zoomed upwards until with a loud "clank" the arched cover of the hoist met the stopping gear at the summit of the elevator. We were at the top of the building.

Like two space explorers under the direction of mission control we stepped off our tiny vehicle on to the diminished space of the top floor. We were at the base of the cubicle of the building. From the ground this part of the structure appeared to be the size of a large birdhouse.

"Geez, it's big enough to live in!" exclaimed Albert.

"Let's take a look out of the window," I said. Dusting the grimy pane with the sleeve of my shirt and standing on our tip-toes we were able to peer through the spot I'd cleared.

"Holy cow, don't look down," I advised, feeling a dizzy sensation in my stomach as I noticed the tin roof of the office like the top of a dog house below us. For the first time in our lives Albert and I saw a portion of the Banner Hall community from a new perspective. Stowers' farm a half mile away looked near enough that if we jumped we could land right in their strawpile. The Brewer cemetery with its gravestones almost a mile down the road looked like a child's sandbox with dominoes standing upright. A farmer was cultivating his summerfallow with a six-horse outfit. They looked like toys. The whole experience was mind-boggling. We must have stood there for five minutes exchanging little more conversation than "Ooh, lookit there!" and "Wow, what a view!" Neither of us were bothered about the time for Uncle Bert's coffee break running out. It occurred to us that we'd better get down.

"Release the brake and let's pull up on the lines!" Albert commanded feeling temporarily the heady joy of power. We had both climbed aboard the small platform and expected that our weight would gently lower the hoist encouraged by the added pull on the ropes. Nothing happened. We were stationary. "Release the brake!" Albert reiterated.

"I've got both feet on the damn thing!" I said flustered, "and I'm pulling like hell. How about you doing something!" Kids around Banner Hall never swore unless the occasion demanded throwing all caution to the winds. We were now in one of those desperate situations.

"What're we going to do if your Uncle Bert comes back?" Albert sighed in remorse. The intoxicating sensation of power was fast receding. The dual captained space ship of Buck Rogers was rapidly returning to the reality of two rather small boys caught on the horns of their own dilemma. Those little demons that excited and inspired us prior to our take off were now returning to taunt us and render us feelings of helplessness and futility. The fruit of the garden turned out once again not to be the great knowledge-giver but exposed our nakedness and dependence. We felt awful.

Our options narrowed. We considered finding something heavy but portable to add to our weight. But on this small platform there was nothing but dust and bird droppings. We examined the ladder that was really nothing but a long row of boards nailed up the side of the wall. They were dangerously slippery because of the silty dust accumulated over the years. I peered warily down through the hole out of which this ladder extended. It was a disquieting view. The decks below outlined the ladder like a series of rings, each descending level a shade darker than the first. Our audaciousness and bravado had now completely left us. We were two very little boys, alone and terrified, with growing feelings of panic. What if we should never get down?

"Why didn't you check this damn thing when we were eight feet up?" I shouted at Albert.

"You were the big shot with your foot on the brake!" he reprimanded me.

"Okay, wise guy, who was lording it over who up here when we landed in the Buck Rogers' space ship," my usually good Grade eight grammar was slipping.

Both of us realized at once that this growing animosity towards each other was not one of the viable options. There must be a better alternative.

"Uncle Bert," I gasped. "We forgot about good old Uncle Bert and his coffee break. We're not alone Albert, old friend; we're in trouble with Uncle Bert, that's true, but we're not going to die up here and have our bones discovered in twenty years. He's going to be looking for us."

"How long do you think it'll be before he notices we're not around or notices that the lift has gone up?" he wondered.

"Well, if he has some suspicions about us trying out some of his Exports behind one of the bins he'll be around fast. He sure watches out for fires. That's why he keeps the weeds and grass from growing up close to the building."

We paced around the floor kicking little dust drifts as we walked. Gazing out the little porthole didn't quite have the same appeal as it did earlier. We'd assimilated the first flush of seeing such a large segment of our world in one view. Now the panorama only reminded us that we were prisoners a long way above the ground. And nobody told us it was a good idea. The elevator was in silence and we seemed so alone and forgotten. An hour or more dragged by.

The late afternoon sun had made this cubicle as hot as the head of the Statue of Liberty on a July day. Our bodies were soaked with sweat, partially from the heat and partially from the growing realization that perhaps our earlier panic may have pointed to some reality. We may be up here for quite awhile.

"Might as well sit down and wait," said Albert, blowing a clear spot on the boards. The dust rose up all around and felt gritty as some of it worked into our perspiring pores. I followed his example. We sat there like a couple of punished school children not verbalizing our resentment but clearly showing our annoyance with the world as it was constructed at that minute.

Moments crept into another hour. We were on the verge of tears.

A door banged in the superstructure away below us. "Boys!" we could hear Uncle Bert's voice. "Boys, where are you? It's getting close to suppertime. Boys!"

We were on our feet in a second. "Here, Uncle Bert, up here!" we both yelled almost in unison. It was almost as if we'd been practicing the response to a call we knew we were going to hear and we would answer it as readily as the prodigal son repeated the speech he had so carefully rehearsed when returning to his father.

"Where? Where in the world are you?" his voice was getting closer as he spoke so that the final words resounded up the shaft, "You're not climbing around on those beams are you?" Then, "Oh, my gosh!" When he said that, we knew that he had noticed the empty space where the lift rested. Uncle Bert never used profanity to my knowledge. He always expressed the opinion that if a person couldn't express himself articulately without resorting to foul language he shouldn't speak. He was being tested now by his own standards.

"What in heaven's name are you two young rascals doing up there?" We knew he was peering up the shaft attempting to determine how far we'd gone, undoubtedly hoping we were only part way up.

"Uncle Bert!" I shouted. "We knew we shouldn't do it and we were only going to try it for a couple of feet, but with one thing and another, up she went," I paused. "We're at the top, I think," I was still not so glad to be rescued that I forgot my fear of being severely reprimanded by one of the most respected elders in the whole Banner Hall community, almost next to Mr. Thompson.

"Oh, Good Lord, give us strength," we heard Uncle Bert mumble. "Look, boys; don't do anything. Just wait. Don't be afraid now," he called up. "I have to go and put on a pair of running shoes and overalls. I'll be right back. You're going to be all right, just stay put." That made us feel really bad. His initial anger had turned to caring compassion already. Only a man with deep resources could be so kind.

"Maybe he's acting nice until he gets us down," Albert suggested. But I knew good old Uncle Bert.

UP THE ELEVATOR SHAFT

"No, Albert: he's forgiven us already. I guess he must have been a really bad kid or something, but he sure understands us. No, he'll climb all the way up that rickety, dusty, bird-manured ladder, and he'll just say, 'Come on, now, you first,' and he'll take one of us down and be right back up for the other of us. We're okay now, and you know what? Our parents will never know." Albert nodded his head in amazement. There are only one or two Uncle Berts in any one community.

Why then, did we keep testing his endurance, like the night we stole the handcar?

It was one of those delicious early fall evenings when the first frost hadn't yet arrived but the clear air had hints of a crispness just around the corner. Albert and I had visited my uncle and aunt after school and after supper we made like we were headed home because we had home work to do. But first we wanted to take a look at the jigger used by the local sectionman.

The sectionman and his family lived just across the tracks from the grain elevator in the Brewer station house. About half a mile south of the siding towards the Melville end of the tracks across the road allowance was the little jigger shed that housed a motor-driven jigger and a hand car. Albert and I had often stood beside the tracks in silent admiration of the men whose privilege it was to operate these magnificent machines. The "putt-putt" of the jigger enjoyed the same kind of distinction soundwise as did the "whoo-oo" of the old prairie separators; both melodic sounds of an era suddenly replaced by the more discordant, stertorous sounds of the more sophisticated technological descendants. One of my older sisters when asked by Mr. Thompson what she wanted to be when she got through school and got out on her own replied without hesitating, "A jigger woman." I admired her for that honest answer. There was truly something praiseworthy about that kind of ambition.

We walked barefoot on the rails. The colder evenings of the late summer didn't alter our lifestyle as far as footwear was concerned until there was a real threat of an unseasonal snow. All the kids went barefoot throughout the better portion of the summer. To go discalced was in style and most important it matched the economy of the day. The soles of our feet became almost impregnable. The cutaneous and subcutaenous layers of skin were as tough as pigskin, enough to give any shoemaker vocational shock. The combined coolness of the evening and the cold steel tracks felt enervating as our feet slid along the rails towards the jigger shack. Through the obscurity of the deepening dusk we could see the outline of one of the machines. It was the handcar. The jigger was in for the night behind the padlocked door of the shed. The handcar sat perpendicular to the main railroad on the tracks that led into the shack.

The moon was beginning to assume its authority over the night. Slight shadows were appearing outlining the bushes, telephone poles and the shape of the small building. The stillness of the evening was broken by the collie barking by Stauers' barn just over the knoll from where we were and the crunch of the gravel beneath our feet. We spoke in tones to match the aura of our surroundings and the mood of our intentions. Although we hadn't actually verbalized the latter both of us knew what we were going to do.

"It looks bigger somehow when you're right next to it like this," whispered Albert.

"Yeah. Look at the length of those arms and handles on the thing that pushes 'em along," I commented, "it's no wonder that it looks easier when you got two guys pumping 'em."

Touching and pushing and poking are God-given inclinations which all boys know about. They use them to test the durability of machines, toys, bikes and other boys. There is absolutely no way these inclinations can be suppressed and few ways through which they can be re-channeled. A cat must test out his claws; a smart pet owner will recognize this threat to his furniture and buy a scratching pole, a boy must poke and explore until his urges are expressed. The handcar was by virtue of this phenomenon being pushed back and forth after the blocks were removed from behind the wheels. A faint squealing sound emanated from the spots where the steel rolled against steel.

One of us sooner or later had to put into words what we both wanted to do. Human nature demands that illicit acts already in their initial stages must be given some structure by verbalization. A man and a woman entering into the action portion of an adultery, for example, have to say something, finally, even it it's postponed to the first tackle or the breath-taking clench. One of the two must say something like, "Oh, my God, what are we doing?" which gives recognition to the reality of the occasion or, "Let's have a weekend", which officially sets the proposition or, "We both know this is bigger than both of us", which sets a neat rationale. For Albert and me and the handcar it was I who finally framed the enterprise with, "Look, there are not supposed to be any trains now, let's see if she'll roll on the tracks."

"Good idea," enjoined Albert, but we gotta be careful of the sound."

We puffed and jostled and shoved until we lifted the front end of the car over the first track and fitted the two metal wheels into place. Then we staggered around until the rear end was lifted into place.

The silence of the evening was broken now but we didn't care. We were making all the noise which as far as we were concerned made the whole night suddenly come to life as if the sounds came from all over. We hopped onto our new oversized toy and with a railroader's "All aboard!" began pumping up and down on the handbar. The car began to move and picked up momentum as we rolled along. Over the road allowance, past the section sign, up beside the grey loading platform where boxcars were loaded and unloaded from farmers' wagons and trucks. Here we halted as suddenly as we had started. A man with a flash light summoned by our simple exuberance and over-indulgence jumped aboard with us.

"Boys, for heaven's sake, what next?" said an exasperated Uncle Bert. For him it must have been very near the breaking point of a great friendship. For Albert and me it was another experience of trust in an elder. The reprimand was to the point and simple. The relationship was saturated with understanding and compassion. As simply as the handcar was returned and parked, two boys were sent homeward, knowing in their hearts it would never be mentioned again. And we knew in our hearts, also, that adult guarantors like Uncle Bert were maybe only one per community.

BROTHERLY LOVE

When I think of manure I think of my brother. That's not because he's any more noisome or malodorous than the next guy. Actually he's been known to be overly sensitive about his personal hygienic care and meticulous about things like getting proper food, ample fresh air and exercise. As a matter of fact, he used to get the rest of us who shared the bedroom to retire early because of his zeal to get the window open even in the dead of winter. He felt there should be ample supplies of oxygen for the three or four inhabitants of that small room. He ate an apple just before hopping under the blankets and always set a glass of water beside his pillow in the event of a sudden need for washing down any virus that he felt approaching him. In the freezing weather the glass was usually full of solid ice by morning.

The association in my mind between my brother and manure grows out of a conflict psychologists sometimes refer to as sibling rivalry. Being a few years my senior, he, I suspected, gained unfair advantage over me in relation to our parents and he assumed that because I was younger I received more consideration than I deserved. The argument never was articulated in direct terminology but usually evolved through a series of minor symbols and acts to fairly hefty tokens like the exchanging of corporal blows or to that which was the ultimate in insult, the scurrilous act of throwing soft cow manure at each other.

This is the way it worked. Dad sent the two of us off to clean the barn. This involved hitching up a team of horses to a hay rack which was drawn in as close as possible to the cowbarn door. With five-pronged manure forks the droppings of the cattle were scraped up and loaded aboard the rack for delivery to a stubble field where we spread it on the land. We knew it was the best type of fertilizer because of its nutritious and roughage value. The operation, although not savory, was simple enough. With a little cooperation and lots of industriousness it wasn't too protracted an exercise. But we normally mixed enough antagonism and disceptation in the undertaking to make it noisy as well as laborious.

"It's your turn to harness the horses, brat," Doug began.

"Spoiled kid, how about you doing your share for a change?" I charged. And off we went. After a rising exchange of countercharges we each ended up harnessing one horse, something we both knew we'd do anyway.

"Okay, get a move on and get that horse out here; we haven't got all day!" Doug had already led Trixie toward the barn's double doors. Trixie was more his temperament, alert and ready to kick out at any unsuspecting passerby. I dragged Pat along mumbling, "C'mon, old sorehead's showing off again." Pat was not unlike my slaver, less mean disposition.

We snapped the reins together joining the horses' heads by the bits fastened to their halters. Doug picked up the reins and gave out his customary "Hi-dee-yodel-ay-hoo!" snapping the reins and galloping the team to their place over the sleigh pole having no problem keeping up with the startled horses.

"Get the lead out!" he yelled back at me trailing along with the two forks dragging ten parallel lines in the snow. I estimated my speed to be equivalent to his getting the team hitched to the double tree and ready to go.

Doug yelled, "Giddup" and with reins in hand executed a rotating leap landing in the middle front of the rack. I threw the forks on the deck and grabbed the retreating back end of the vehicle looping my arms around the planks with my feet planted securely through the holes at the bottom. This fling around the yard in the snow was one of the most enjoyable features of barn cleaning. It was useful in warming up the team as well as giving the arduous task of manure hauling a more alluring appeal. By trotting and galloping the horses the full circumference of the farmyard we enjoyed four terrific crack-the-whip sensations when the corners were sharply negotiated. My position at the extreme end of the motion gave me the thrilling equivalent of any two-bit ride at the Yorkton exhibition.

Slowing the horses down to a slow trot and then a walk, Doug parked the rack in front of the cowbarn door. "Let's shake a leg!" he shouted at me as he unlatched the old door under the low-hanging eaves. The steam rolled out of the opening as the hot, wet air from the interior clashed with the cold crisp atmosphere outside. "Why does he always act like such a big whore?" I grumbled under my breath.

The gutters at the cows' posteriors were loaded with straw-laced fresh manure slopped into gallons of urine. We stuck our forks into the piles closest to the door and carried chunks of dripping goo to the opening and hoisted each forkful onto the deck. Some of the liquid ran through the spaces between the boards and some of it froze as soon as it touched the boards. Making the first space in the gutter was the biggest task. Then with the help of a garden hoe used for scraping the more liquid residue into the straw and droppings on either side, Doug and I moved further away from each other as the job progressed.

"Pretty nice job Dad give you," I said not being able to stand the longer than usual break in the conversation and smarting a little as I thought about how he was always telling me to get a move on, "letting you do the chopping in a nice warm granary while I had to dig straw out of the stack."

"Listen punk, Dad knows who to trust with the expensive and complicated machinery. Quit feeling like a spoiled brat and shut your mouth; look how much more I've loaded than you, the stuff's all running from your end to mine!" Why did he always start those accusations, I wondered. I seethed inside, knowing that he was right.

"Okay, cow's turd, my fork's smaller and my leg's sore; I can't always be the fastest," I lied on both counts. Gee I felt mad. What'll I say now? Before I could follow up, Doug gave his customary derisive whoop, "Haw, haw! Listen to poor little momma's boy making excuses again. Can't keep up to a man, so he's got to invent little notions." Now I could cheerfully bust his head; but, I'd wait.

The gutter was finally cleared. Doug held up his fork threateningly behind a cow with her tail raised. "Hold it in for ever or let it all out now!" he laughed, "otherwise I'll smack you in the behind." Why did he have to act like he was enjoying himself, I asked myself. "Let's get this load of next year's bumper crop out before it all runs through the boards," he joked as we stuck our forks into the juicy mound in the centre of the rack. I took up my station on the back and Doug grabbed the reins. The horses yanked the sleigh runners loose from their frozen tracks and broke into a slow trot. With bells jingling and hooves sounding hollow on the ice, we were off to the open field where the wind cut rows of shadowy drifts across the frost inlaid landscape. The icy nip in the air had little effect on my vindictive feelings towards my brother. As we moved through deeper snow and the horses slowed to a determined walk, I jumped off the back to warm my toes, letting my feet thump through the manure-stained mocassins on the hard surface. I'd warm a little and think of some kind of revenge for the day.

"Whoah!" commanded the teamster. The sleigh stopped and I climbed back on and took up my position behind the steaming mound. We began weaving a brown, spattered pattern across the glistening snow; the horses, well-trained for this purpose, moved ahead and paused, responding to a single "click click" of the driver's tongue and a quiet "whoah." Now I would introduce a carefully prepared barb into the proceedings.

"Say, dumbbell," we rarely used each other's names except when reporting some misdeameanor to our parents, "I guess mom gave you the devil for punching her loaves down this morning, eh?" I had seen Doug after breakfast poking at the rising loaves which mother had carefully set out under tea towels in preparation for the oven. He hadn't been doing any real damage to them, just sort of pinching and pulling at the dough like a younger boy might do out of a sense of curiosity. It would have gone unnoticed and unharmed if I hadn't spotted him and squealed, "Hey mom, look what Doug's doing to your bread!" Mother, always attentive to this kind of ominous warning, was quick to come through the door from the dining room to the kitchen just as Doug was lowering a corner of the tea towel over the pinched spot on the rising loaf. With eight kids to supervise throughout her homemaker's career, she could not be blamed for occasionally drawing premature conclusions. Doug indeed looked guilty. I had laid what appeared to be a water-tight charge.

"You little brat, get your hands off that dough!" she exclaimed, rushing towards him with arms outstretched for the grab.

"Look, ma," we used that term of helpless endearment when we knew for sure we were on her side, "he's pulled a big chunk out of one corner." I lifted one towel a little, knowing she wouldn't verify my accusation at this point.

"You dirty little liar; shut your ever-gobbling mouth," Doug raised his voice. "Mom, he isn't telling the truth. Just look and see!" She didn't wait for any more explanation. Doug was grabbed and severely clouted on the back of the head with an adept hand. He was kicked in the trousers with a really swift left foot. I giggled just enough that he noticed but not openly so that mother would behold only a shocked expression on my face. This really did the trick. Doug shook himself free of mother's grip on his arm and rounded the table in pursuit of me feigning much fear. I whirled around behind mother with pleas of "Help ma!" rising from my lips. She picked up the kitchen broom and walloped Doug a good one on the rear end. Now almost in tears he was losing control of his actions. I gloated. He was cut down. Running over to the cupboard he threw the towels onto the floor and began flailing at the well-rounded, rising dough with both fists. I was jubilant. He got a real thrashing with the broom and ran outside crying openly.

In the interval between then and now I had my face washed in the icy snow and my cap thrown into the cat dish. I was still a little afraid of him out here in the field but was more annoyed at his uncanny ways of making me feel inferior to him in everything we did together around the yard like cleaning the barn. Now the reminder of the bread dough frame-up was all I needed to get the old prickles going again.

"Boy you're small," he sneered. "Can't stand up for yourself in normal ways so have to tell lies and invent little wormy schemes. God, you're hateful." He threw the forkful he had in his hand with a little more zest so that the spattery pattern extended beyond the outer edge of the line we were designing in the snow.

"Doug, honest," I jested, "I wouldn't have said anything, but I really thought you were spoiling mom's loaves. I didn't think she'd get so mad."

"Rotten pig," he pronounced, "lie in the beginning and you lie in the end. You've got no character; you stink!"

"You be careful how you talk," I threatend, "or I'll bash you one!" I was still relatively safe behind a fair-sized mound of cow manure. Besides if he should dart across to my end I could hop over the side and run. He was in charge of the team.

"You talk so big all the time. You never give me a chance. Half the time Mom and Dad think I'm stupid because you've had your chance to beat me to them. Besides, I hate your filthy guts." It's really quite remarkable what brothers can say to each other with full-fraught feelings. Hurts may be buried deep but not for long in this kind of comminication. There were many times when we unloaded hostility mutually in this open manner. But then it was done; we felt understood and clean. The more remarkable phenomenon is that if some outsider like some neighbor's kid was to pick on either of us we'd fight tooth and nail to protect each other.

One time I was so furious with Doug I decided I'd make him dance like I saw a cowboy make an Indian dance in a show at the Princess Theatre in Melville. Doug had bugged me and tormented me with verbal threats and obscene gestures all day. I was completely flabbergasted.

He was fixing a pump at the dugout and had called for me to come and help him raise the thing out of the well. He called in that same vexatious, antagonizing voice, "Hey stupid! Get out here fast. I need a lift on this thing — Hurry up now, move it for a change!" I hated that command. I'd get him now. He'd be laboring under the weight of the pump. I ran to the tool shed where we kept the .22 rifle in the summer, scooped up a handful of bullets and entered the bush by the dugout from the opposite side where he stood tugging at the apparatus and looking down the road where he'd expect to see me approaching. "Okay", I said to myself, "go ahead and holler at me some more." I didn't have to wait long.

"C'mon you old stud! Get out here. I know you're just playing little doll games. Hurry up or I'll drop this thing and come and wring your little chicken neck!"

That's what I wanted to hear. Standing up at the edge of the bush I used my best Hopalong Cassidy voice, "Dance you bareskinned savage!" I ordered and aimed the rifle a couple of yards to one side of his feet and fired, then a little closer on the other side and fired, then a bit closer in front and fired, "Dance, you bugger!" I shouted. Doug dropped the pump and ran. Provoked animosity leads to larger and larger tokens of retribution. It aids in the process, also to depersonalize your brother to the image of the much beleaguered redskin of that day or his counterpart today the abused foreigner and person we don't understand because we haven't got to know him. However, I loved my brothers.

Now out here in the open field another side of these feelings were fomenting again.

"You coward," Doug answered my response, "you can't ever deal with me directly. You're always using dramatized scenes and setting me up for somebody else to hurt me. You should grow some of your own guts. By the way I don't know what you've got in mind now, but if you think we've evened up for that little incident this morning you've got another think coming. I'll get you for that yet." He was getting really steamed up. I enjoyed that and threw in a little more ammunition.

"Boy, you're big on the lip! You're so dumb you can't even think ahead. I get you caught all the time. You know big boy, you're a jackass and a freak all rolled up together." I flung a fork well beyond the pattern. "Gee, I can even throw manure farther than you!"

"Big deal, he goes through life being the greatest manure spreader of all time. Nice going little guy, but watch this!" He heaved a tremendously large forkful into the air simulating my recent execution from one end of the extension to the other. I guess this is what started one of the dirtiest outdoor sports I've ever participated in. I threw a forkful over the top of the rack. Doug let go with another that made a half circle and landed in a spray and a spatter on the back of the rack and part of my overalls.

"Careful kid," I warned as I jerked a little turd off the heap and let it roll over his foot.

"Careful yourself," he replied, and returned the gesture only increasing the volume and velocity just a bit. A hardened chunk of excretion hit my leg.

"Take this one home," I replied angrily and flipped a forkful of straw in his direction so that he was forced to duck.

"You dirty punk," was hurled at me with a hefty sized forkful of straw riddled with warmer dung. Pieces of feculence and water ran down the bib of my overalls.

"Okay, beast!" and I dug my fork into the softest pile of excrement I could find and hurled it at Doug. What a strike! He was dripping from head to foot and the force of the blow pushed him against the front of the rack. The battle was now beyond the terms of an eye for an eye and a tooth for a tooth. No quid-pro-quo relationship now. It was fullscale vengeance with all the stops out. The mound of manure dissipated as the two combatants, the rack and backs of the horses were the recipients of a cloudburst of dripping, gooey, chewed-up cow defecation. We stood there exhausted, facing each other, dribbling overalls, caps and mocassins absolutely saturated with warm stinking semi-fluid. We had poured out all our wrath and pent-up hostility. Only stupid half-grins spread through the murky disgrace of our faces. War had once more spent itself and neither of us really was victor. How were we going to explain this to the real loser of the battle: mother?

WARM RAIN AND UNIFORMS

This Friday night dance at Banner Hall was going to be a special one for me. All week I'd been telling the boys in Grade eight at Runneberg School that my sister's boyfriend was on a three day leave from the army and he'd be bringing my sister to the dance. Maybe he'd wear his uniform. He was a Captain in the Army Supply Corps. It mattered less to me what branch he represented. I'd seen that uniform the only other time he'd been at our place. He was waiting between trains and had a couple of hours to slip out and see my sister and meet my folks for the first time. The hard, peaked cap and leather-trimmed khakis were what I'd noticed most.

Uniforms had a strange anagogic power over me and my friends. Because of the war and the prevalence of service personnel from the nearby air base in Yorkton we'd seen a fair number of non-commissioned personnel and grew accustomed to their rig but officers were scarce around Banner Hall. A man in the navy blue and gold braid of the Royal Canadian Navy and the Air Force blue of the flyer and khaki of the army elicited a kind of awe in us. These, after all, were the men who epitomized the images of grandiose glory in our minds when victory bond rallies were held in Banner Hall. Albert and I and the rest of the grade eights had been at several of those rallies when Judge Mackay of Melville stirred the assembled crowd with tales of heroism and songs of the glories of war. In his home-grown lyric tenor voice he stirred in us feelings of nationalistic fervor and wartime romance with songs such as "It's A Long Way To Tipperary, "There's A Long, Long Road A-Winding," "Praise The Lord And Pass The Ammunition" and an original song that included a line something like, "One Canuck is worth a Yank and a dozen Jerks." Then after a pitch for War Savings Certificates and Government Victory Bonds we'd all raise our voices in total abandonment in the fervor-filled lines:

"Get on, get on, get on the road to victory
And buy another bond today!"

Men in uniform symbolized our hopes for the much-used terms 'freedom' and 'democracy'. Men in officers' clothes evoked a response of breathless admiration. I wanted my classmates to know that my sister's boyfriend would be at the dance and I had to make sure he'd wear his uniform.

One of the things that was beyond my understanding is that when a serviceman had three days away from the base the last thing he wanted to wear was his uniform. It seemed odd to me that this was the case. How such resplendent garb that commanded so much respect could be looked upon by the wearer with obvious disdain was beyond my understanding. Somehow I'd think of a way to communicate this without revealing the fact that by wearing his uniform to the dance he'd make me into a temporary hero in the eyes of my classmates.

My sister had served coffee and sandwiches to Orest shortly after his arrival. I had just come home from school and gulped down three remaining chicken sandwiches.

"Do you have chores to do or what?" he said, intimating by the sound of his voice that maybe he'd be interested in following me about the tasks I had to fulfill before supper.

"Yeah; I have to feed the chickens, gather the eggs and fill the woodbox," I said expectantly.

"Would you like a little help?" he offered.

"Sure," I replied. "It won't take long. Then we can play catch." I could see a really live opportunity opening up to lead into what was really burning inside of me. Orest was dressed in casual civvy slacks and an open neck shirt. I knew he wouldn't be wearing that to the dance so he'd be changing anyway.

We walked to the chicken house together. He asked about school and about my chores. I wondered how I was going to get around to talking about the dance tonight and what we'd all be wearing. Thinking back to it now, it occurs to me that my questions must have sounded pretty obvious. After we'd picked up two wheelbarrow loads of split wood and I got the softball and glove from the back porch, I opened with, "I guess everybody will be really dressed up for the dance tonight."

"You mean it's some kind of special affair?" he asked.

I stationed myself in front of the garage doors and put on the glove so that he would pitch. "Not that much different than usual; but around Banner Hall people don't have that much to do. So when there's a dance everybody sort of tries to outdo the other. Then there are always quite a few soldiers and airmen around. They get looked up to a lot by the rest of the people. I guess it's because all of us around here know they're protecting our country and everything. All us kids really admire them." I caught a curving pitch in my glove and returned the ball with an underhand loop.

"I suppose you can tell who the soldiers are by the fact that they're strangers," said Orest. I have suspicions now that maybe he'd caught on already and was egging me on for his own enjoyment. But I didn't know then. I really thought that he was a trifle slow.

"Oh no, there are always lots of people we don't know. People come to these dances from as far south as Killaly and west from Fenwood. There are many strangers. The servicemen always wear their uniforms, of course, which makes them stand out from the rest of the crowd." I might as well go all the way now, "That's why they like coming to our dances. They're treated with more respect and honor. I've never seen a serviceman standing in line with his girl to get to the ticket window. They're always invited to the head of the line. The same at lunch time, the orchestra leader always calls out, 'Get your partners for the lunch time waltz. Soldiers, sailors and airforce men, you're first.' Then the music starts and all the 'uniformed' people," I emphasized the word, "are the first ones on the floor while everybody stands up and claps. Then they dance with their girls around the floor and before others are allowed to dance these couples are ushered to the lower hall where they're the first to be served." I returned the ball again after a stinging pitch which would have registered as a strike at a ball game. Thinking I was making my point very well I added the clinches, "But, of course, if the guy isn't in uniform he's just one of the farmers." After another couple of pitches I added, "Officers are very scarce around here and when they go in uniform they really get treated well."

I never knew why Orest, to my delight and my friend's open-mouthed admiration, wore his uniform to that dance. Had he intended to all along? Did he have no other dress clothes? Did he do it to impress my sister? Did the army demand that the uniform be worn? I'll never know. But I have a sneaking hunch about it.

For some reason we always picked stones on Saturday. Whenever my brothers and sisters brought their courting friends home to meet the folks a zigzagging trek across one of the summer fallowed fields seemed to be one of the obligations confronting their weekend schedule. Stonepicking is one of life's necessary evils on the prairies. Prior to the mechanized stone-picking machines of recent years the modus operandi involved the simple but arduous task of following a flat-bottomed wagon drawn by a team of horses and hand picking and loading the rocks from their perch on the land. Most of them could be wrestled aboard by single manpower but occasionally a crowbar was needed to pry larger stones out of the ground and logging chains attached to the wagon were used to drag them to the stone pile at the fence line dividing the quarter sections. It's a dusty, sweaty, hand-blistering, back-breaking operation. It was always a great source of amusement for the younger of us to observe one of our sister's new boy friends garbed in coveralls feign enthusiasm for the task as we rumbled across the field to the stone-strewn hills.

Orest had risen early. The music of the dance of the night before must have still been thumping in his head. The entire sky's deep blue and the sun's penetrating rays announced a hot July day. Bacon and eggs had been served for breakfast; this always signalled heavy work ahead.

"The army keeps us physically fit," he raised his voice, which quavered because of the bouncing wagon and so that it would be heard above the clattering of the planks that wiggled and jumped and rubbed together on the wagon, "This stone picking should be a snap for me," he said to Dad who was driving the team. My brother and I sitting at the rear of the vehicle with our feet dangling over the end gave each other a poke and a knowing look. It would be a tantalizing and entertaining day. We'd get dirty and tired but at least have some amusement off and on throughout the grueling process.

Seasoned stone pickers did not start the job suddenly as if rushing would shorten the agony of the enterprise. It was better to take it easy at first and allow your arms and legs to accustom themselves to the dead weight of the rocks. Walking slowly and exercising the arms in a swinging fashion, hitting your gloves together to keep the circulation going and the muscles taut was the kind of stance to develop. Newcomers and especially those intent on impressing observers often erred in jumping off the wagon, running to the first rocks and with three or four of them piled up carried the armful to the wagon. This drained the energy and stretched the muscles into painfully hot nerve tissue in a very short time.

"Take it easy, Orest, you'll hurt yourself going at it like that," Dad warned after the horses stopped and we began pacing between the rocks and the wagon. Orest had jumped athletically to the ground and trotted briskly over to some scattered rocks about the size of large coconuts. We were carrying single stones, he was bunching them and clearing impressive spaces at each sweep. The early hour in the day and his desire to excel at this task had combined to thrust him into the unenviable position of a recruit for early Saturday exhaustion.

"It's okay; nothing to it," he hopped back and forth.

After three loads of rocks had been gathered and dumped, my brother and I reflected with experience on what was happening. Orest was beginning to tire noticeably. Perspiration ran down his face and his shirt was muddy from the accumulated moisture and grime. His earlier erect posture had deteriorated into a pitiful pretzel-like walk. But his spirit and stamina remained firm. Although he was now walking slower with his feet making little scoop marks in the dry soil, he was still picking up two or three stones at a time. All the while he kept up a running conversation with Dad about the war, life in the army and prospects for peace. Dad often paused and sat on the edge of the platform while listening or adding a comment, and observed this young man's grit and industriousness with unexpressed admiration. He knew, however, that the time for intervention was near. We knew it was a matter of brief time before Dad would bring this painful experience to a close. Maybe we'd quit early or change jobs where Orest's exit could be made expediently and with honor.

Another hour went by and two more loads were delivered. Also, three huge rocks had been pulled from the earth's clutches with crowbar and chain. Orest was wilting. His arms appeared wilted and his voice sounded fragile as the conversation continued.

"Guess we better pull over to that slough and let these mares have a drink," Dad announced. This gave my brother and me a chance to drag our bare feet in the water when the horses splashed across the pond. We had quenched our own thirsts a half dozen times from a gallon jug of water wrapped in moistened sacking, now it was the horses' turn. Orest backed gingerly toward the side of the plank fronting his side of the wagon. With blistered hands and aching arms he lifted himself aboard. My brother and I listened for and heard a suppressed groan. The wagon rumbled towards the slough.

The enticing freshness of the water clear to the bottom of the pond, Orest's aching, tortured limbs and his torrid, blistered hands compounded by the intense heat of the day and the results of the revelry of the preceding night at Banner Hall combined to precipitate in him an inevitable reaction. After the horses stopped and the stillness of that magic moment was broken only by the slurping of thirsty animals sucking up water around their bits, Orest emitted a weird groan that began low in his chest and grew to a whoop when it burst from his lips, and with arms flung skyward he leapt headlong into the freshness of his surroundings. Splashing and groaning, he rolled over and over letting every pain, every itch in his aching body soothe to a harmonious oneness in the cleansing, healing water. We observed this therapeutic scene with quiet understanding, my brother and I saving our bursts of laughter for later in the day, and Dad finally said when the splashing ceased, "Maybe you'd like to head over to the house to get cleaned up a bit. You've had enough for today. Thanks for your help." With that face-saving facilitative directive, he snapped the lines, sending the rest of us back into the field for more rocks.

Two hours afternoon sleep in the shade of a huge maple tree in our back yard renewed Orest's energy for Saturday evening. Romance blossomed in our living room after the rest of the family went upstairs to bed. Mother put the evening's plans for us kids into perspective when she announced at supper,

"It's been a big day; what with last night's dance and the little sleep you kids got plus all of today's work you're all tired." Looking directly into the eyes of each of us and politely but resolutely slanting her head towards Orest and our second oldest sister she said, "They'll be wanting to do some visiting in the living room and won't want you breaking up the conversation by your traipsing around the house. Now after supper, get out and get your chores done, then get your baths and off to bed without a lot of fuss." We all knew what she meant. We did feel tired, but even if we weren't ready for rest we understood the futility of counterargument tonight. Her mind was made up and she was making it easier for us to accept peace with honour.

The stairway to the upper floor of our house led up from the living room. This meant that once we got up to bed, with people in the living room and the door at the foot of the stairs closed you were retired for the night. Trips to the outhouse and my brother's need for a glass of water next to his pillow and other necessary arrangements in anticipation of a long summer night's slumber had better be executed in advance of the final trip upstairs. We went to bed. A peaceful silence enshrouded the house. Crickets chirped and frogs croaked in harmony outside. Only the whispering voices of the couple in the living room injected the sign of life inside. It was a dreamy, heavenly kind of atmosphere. But this paradisiac state could not prevail for long. The odds against its prolonged existence were stacked by too many unvariables. Factors such as a boys' room literally filled with curious, youthful boyish energy next door to their sisters' devilment disguised with innocence, next door to parents whose voices could rule the roost with a threatening, "Settle down in there!" created conditions for puckishness and rather good-natured, mischief-making. The trick was for one person to stir up enough trouble to instigate trouble and remain blameless. If one boy could, through a cleverly devised scheme, gradually and persistently provoke his bed mate into venting his hostility in a loud voice or get him into a fit of uncontrollable giggles, then by quickly turning on his side and feigning sleep, the call or the visit from the master bedroom would be directed towards the victim. Or if the mood was right for a more major scolding, the boys could incite the girls to riot or call out for help. Tonight, because of the general pressure applied by mother for a non-eventful slumber, the group of us brothers and sisters suppressed our usual tendencies to provoke the others to a state of uninhibited behavior where they'd get caught. But this kind of suppression leads to unexpected energy leaks.

We were not quiet long. One of us, unable to resist breaking the oppressive silence, simulated a giant's snore that rasped and sputtered through the hallway and down the stairs. This provoked a couple of others to giggle in muffled tones, carefully disguising their identity. Not to be out-acted, two new sonorous gasps and rattles emanated from pillows carefully arched over heads. Then one of my brothers, always willing and prepared to give leadership in this mode of group participation, released a powerfully-perfumed blast of gas from his posterior, the noise of which contrasted dramatically with the faked snores and the smell of which caused his roommates to gasp disapproving "Ooohhs!" and, fanning our pillows around to create a breeze, move our room from tranquility to chaos.

"Cut out that noise!" came Dad's voice.

"Mom, Dad, those boys won't let us sleep!" our sisters were not going to miss this oppotunity.

"Mom, they woke us up," I called out, "they made out they were snoring; you heard them," I accused.

"Dad, that's a lie," shouted Hazel whose ambition in life was to be a jigger lady, "make them quit. We're tired and just want to sleep. Can't help it if we have to work harder than they do." Sisters seem to have a knack of embracing two or three contentious areas in one sweeping statement.

Our oldest brother spoke with authority, "Now listen, Mom and Dad, don't fall for that line again. Those girls came up here tonight intent on getting us guys into trouble. They're doing pretty good but I know you're not going to swallow that technique again." Then in a reconciliatory note he added, "Let's just start all over again. We'll settle down if they do." That was big brotherly enough for everyone to accept.

"Good night Mom and Dad," our voices rose at different times from various places.

"Good night kids; please, settle down," rejoined Mother.

Again silence reigned and was broken again by the staged snoring sound. The entire drama was re-enacted three times before we actually began to settle down. For some reason all of this nonsense placed considerable stress on my dad's bladder. Under normal circumstances he would have relieved himself in the white enamel pot under the bed. Tonight the pot had been left outside. I didn't know about the chain of events until sometime later but I guess it worked out something like this.

The kids had all gone to sleep. My sister and her handsome boy friend whose uniform I adored were engaged in the process of courting and respectable lovemaking in the living room at the foot of the stairs. Dad, after being awakened from that first deep sleep that hits a weary man after a hard day's work, began to feel as if he'd forgotten to look after all the toilet necessities in preparation for bed. At first this didn't bother him much because he knew that if he needed to he could use the pot so close to him that he could reach it under the bed. After settling us kids down with a stern voice he sank quickly back into peaceful slumber. Then we woke him again and again. Each time he felt more like using the pot.

Finally when he was re-awakened and had to actually get out of bed to make threatening sounds with his feet as they approached our bedroom door which was in fact the act that did the trick, we went to sleep. Then he needed that pot. With a weary sigh he reached for it.

"Where's that damn pot?" he whispered, threatened slightly himself.

"It should be there," Mom reassured him. A tired man shows his feelings more readily when his sleep has been disturbed. In a stage whisper he followed up, "That damned pot is not here. Is it over on your side?" Mother then threw herself out of her side of the bed and squatted down to reach under and pull it out for an anxious Dad. Their hands touched underneath the bed.

"Oh dear, I think it's on the back step," Mom breathed suddenly, remembering an unfinished chore.

"I got to use that pot,"Dad fumed mostly in frustration. His bladder now felt as if he hadn't cleared it for days.

"Go back to bed and go to sleep; you'll forget about it. It's your imagination," Mom said, "you always get like this when the kids won't settle down." That wasn't exactly the sort of advice Dad needed now. It upset him more.

"I don't want to go downstairs and parade past those two like as if we're checking on them," he said, "but I've got no choice." Then he added, "What am I going to say, 'Forgot to pee, wife forgot the pot?' I can't do that. She'd never forgive me," Dad was caught between polite considerations, feelings for his daughter and this outrageous pressure that could not be contained much longer.

"Dad you simply cannot go through that living room." Mother affirmed strongly.

"What am I going to do?" It's sad to hear a man caught between panic and

WARM RAIN AND UNIFORMS

necessity. He walked over to the window which overlooked the front porch roof. He raised the window.

Just about the time Mom and Dad were scrimmaging on the floor at the sides of their bed looking for the pot, the happy couple downstairs decided to walk hand in hand through the front door into the veranda. The summer evening air was motionless but enticing. The leaves of the vines that enshrouded the wire netting around the veranda were heavy with dew; a partially veiled moon announced an approaching cloud. It was a quiet peaceful place where two people in love could share little secrets and words of endearment when purportedly except for the crickets and the frogs the rest of the world slept.

Standing there together leaning against the pole that supported the porch roof, arms around waists, the ecstatic pair lingered in time-suspended serenity. An embrace was shared, a kiss enjoyed. This summit of enchantment was disturbed only by a sound not noticed in the preceding moments. There was a distinct drip of water on the wooden step in front of them followed by more drips in increasing volume until a veritable stream broke before their eyes which itself diffused into additional little streams. It temporarily deflected the attention of the couple from each other's eyes to this new phenomenon of the night. Orest put his hand into one of the miniature waterfalls and exclaimed softly, "It's fairly teeming out. What a magnificently beautiful summer shower!"

Reflecting on this some days later I thought this was not very honorable treatment for a man who wore an army captain's uniform.

STAGE FRIGHT

It was slightly more than fortuitous that the opening line of my monologue at the Runneberg School Christmas Concert was from the well-known essay that began, "Whenever I go into a bank I get nervous." That was just about all I uttered before my mind went blank. I couldn't remember what I was standing there for. I saw individuals in the front row gradually merge into the blur of the crowd. I was unaware of what was going on around me; the prompter's voice was merely some annoying static emanating from a great unseen void somewhere behind me; two large gas lanterns hissed above my head; the place was in silence and I had forgotten not only my lines, but my own identity. I had stage fright.

The advantage of being caught in the throes of stage fright is that of the accompanying numbness. I would not blush or giggle uncontrollably or start to cry because of the protective layers of anonymity engendered by the ego during this traumatic experience. Obviously all of the visible and invisible rehearsals merely postponed the grim reality of this stage appearance. In my mind I had gone through the performance over and over again. Actually I had survived the agony of the dress rehearsals and the countless unnerving times I stood beside my desk and rattled through the short address, my voice quavering and my knees knocking to my mortification each time. But I had on each successive trial convinced myself that I was making progress. Although my neck reddened with anxiety and my mouth craved lubrication I did not break down and cry.

Crying in front of my classmates was an infelicity I never wanted repeated again. It was the ultimate humiliation. The first time it happened was in the first week of my first year in school. My pencil had rolled out of the groove on the desk top and on to the floor. I was proud of that pencil with its bright gold and red colors, its large eraser and its length. It was the first time in my life I owned a new pencil. Mom and Dad brought it home one day from Melville with my new scribbler that had the arithmetic tables on the back. I didn't want to use it until school began so it was kept in its shiny condition until the first day when I grasped it avariciously in my hand and guarded it carefully from harm. Now when it hit the floor I envisioned a broken point.

It was worse than that. I leaned out of my desk and attempted to retrieve it. But just as my fingers touched it, it rolled beyond my grasp and under the desk across the aisle. An older boy who was enjoying my discomfiture placed his foot on it and rolled it back and forth beneath his shoe. I could hear the crackling crunch announcing its annihilation. I was shocked and felt desperate in the face of such open cruelty. I started to cry. I didn't want anyone to notice but the more I smothered my sobs, the more the increased pressure broke through my nose and forced my hands away from my mouth. I blubbered and snorted and the sobs broke into uninhibited wails. Now even the sympathetic teacher couldn't bring my open grief back under control before it had run its course.

Having once lost face before your peers it's extremely difficult to replace an undesirable image with a more heroic one. I would have preferred a bully's image to that of a sissy but having cried once it was easier to cry again and again. Hence whenever it was time for voice tests and singing, my spirits sank very low. Fear of making a mistake and being ridiculed often made a fool out of me. When it came my turn to sing, because we had no alternative but to go through the words of an entire song, I frantically requested the teacher to let me do the bee song. It had only two lines and one could get through the entire ditty without varying pitch or key. I marched stifflegged to the front of the class on those crushing occasions, stared dead ahead and proceeded as quickly as possible with:

"Bees gather honey,
Paying poll and money."

Then rushing back to my seat I'd slink down praying that my performance would suffice albeit unsuccessfully. If questioned by my teacher at this point or criticized I'd burst into tears. His practice approximated my art of speechmaking also. Except when speech classes called for my participation, my fear of standing alone before that mixed group of Grades one to ten often caused me to forget subject, text and audience. In the earlier grades, tears were the painful remedy and during the latter grades plain ordinary stage fright resulting in a nonsensical stupor was the manner in which my human organism protected itself from the unfriendly audience.

The blurred figures in the front row were beginning to get restless. Nervous coughs accompanied by scraping winter boots on the floor of Banner Hall were awakening me to my hapless position. This indeed was the Christmas concert. I was one of that class of rugged eighth graders and I was standing before this expectant audience making them as uneasy as hens in a chicken house invaded by a skunk. They were empathizing with me but were unable to do anything to help me. My parents must have felt like dropping through the floor not from shame or disgust but realizing the importance of a breakthrough for me at this point in despair because I'd blown it again.

The lamps hissed on. The prompter's voice broke through my fuzzy trance.

"Start again!" "Whenever I go into a bank I get nervous!" I suddenly regained composure. I felt a surge of self-confidence pervade my entire being such as I had never felt before. My knees steadied, my eyes sparkled with the mild amusement of an orator about to break an original story on his audience, my heart beat loosened to a healthy, regular thump and the palms of my hands dried. I freed my fingers which had been tightened into two little balls and lifted my right arm in a waving gesture. I was amazed at the new sense of freedom that allowed my entire body to relax. Moving my feet from their rigid side by side position I set my left foot just a little ahead of my right, poised for a dramatic address. Lowering my eyes which had been staring glassily above the audience I concentrated on people whose faces began taking shape in the front row where the gas lanterns from the stage cast a few reflections in the darkened hall. Clearing my throat I began,

"Whenever I go into a bank I get nervous." I said it, clearly, distinctly and with the resonance of a CBC announcer. I couldn't believe my ears. Was that really my voice? Did I say that? Even though the words of the great Canadian essayist flowed back into consciousness I felt an indomitable desire to wade into some off the cuff dialogue. I wanted to break into the core of this captive audience and move them off their seats. I wanted to open my being to them and expose all the pent-up philosophy that had been ground out in quiet suffering in erstwhile predicaments when my voice had been choked by fear and shame. Now I wanted to free them in the spirit of my own newly discovered freedom. The gas lamps hissed on. In actual time I'd been standing there for only an embarrassing number of seconds; in the depths of my life I'd been out into eternity and back. I'd go over that line again,

"Whenever I go into a bank I get nervous. Well, maybe you'd get nervous, too, if you didn't have any money in the bank and you had my credit rating and you were going to ask for a loan!" I paused because I figured the farmers could identify with that line I'd just made up and there would be an appreciative response. There was gentle and relieved laughter. That added fuel to my newly discovered self-confidence.

"Well..." I was already developing my own style. The audience appreciated the drawl and showed it with a ripple of laughter.

"Well... the things that go on in banks you wouldn't believe. The last time I was in town I saw this farmer taking a pig into the bank. I went up to him as he was holding the door open and asked why he was taking his pig into the bank. He said he was made to feel nervous in the bank the last time he'd been in because he'd asked for a loan and the manager said he couldn't give him one. He asked the manager why that was the case. The manager told him he didn't have enough security. "You bring home the bacon and share some with this bank and I'll get you a loan. So the man told me he was going to bring some real live bacon in for that unwilling manager."

I paused for laughter because I figured I deserved it. The crowd hollered in joy and stomped their feet and clapped their hands. Actually looking back at it now I see how dumb that joke really was, but I guess they were really pleased with my performance. I was a new person. I noticed Mr. Thompson move from his chair at the side over to one of the centre seats. He couldn't believe it was me.

"Well . . . anyway, whenever I go into a bank I get nervous. You see banks appear to be more than they really are, if you know what I mean." I was plunging into some homespun philosophy the like of which I'd heard the recorded voice of Will Rogers give. It must be his style I wanted to emulate. But where was it going? What was I going to say after this kind of provocative beginning? "You see, it's not really the big door at the front or that row of little cages behind which you see those efficient-looking ladies, that gives you the heeby-jeebees. It's the guy on the other side of that little wooden fence in the office. The manager. He's so good at clearing his throat and saying 'no' that he reminds you of some mean, unhappy uncle you know. You're taught to be scared of him and he knows that. If he ever figures for a moment that you're not scared of him, he closes his door and you can't get in to see him. But most folks don't get that brave; so for most of us who go into banks we get nervous. It's not the money or the place, it's all because of that guy who seems to be what he isn't, you see. So next time you go into a bank and feel nervous, you think of what I'm telling you and when you feel your stomach getting like it was crawling with ants, just march up to one of those wickets and say, "Pardon me ma'am but I want to speak to the manager on an urgent matter." That'll get you in. Then when you get ushered to this guy's door, don't let your scared feelings tell you what to do; listen to me." The direction my monologue was going was engendering amongst my hearers a sympathetic response. The funny part of the monologue with its incongruities between my unsureness and the contrasted over-confidence which let the people laugh in gratitude for my deliverance from complete humiliation was presently giving way to actual interest in the content of what I was saying. Still there were the surprised and mildly shocked and amused faces of my teacher and my peers in the eighth grade who were witnessing the transition from a crowd-frightened milksop to an orator of sorts who enjoyed his new image of crowd-pleaser.

"Don't wait to be invited in; just enter and sit down in the chair opposite his desk as if you owned a good portion of the bank. This will upset the manager a little and will give you the opportunity to move in on him." The words were coming out as if I'd just read the script. I tried not to think of this because I was afraid I'd get lost in my own narration. "He'll likely try to say something about this point, but don't let him. Hush him up by holding your hand up like this." I held up my right hand in a traffic cop's stop signal. "Then rush right out with words such as 'This country's in bad shape. You bankers are letting things get out of hand. You're not keeping up on where the people are and you can't deal with money matters unless you understand where the people are because they're telling you what's important and what's not important in the community. You guys spend too much time behind closed doors. The whole world out there changes a little every time you close that door. I'm here to help you before it's too late for you to do anything about it.' By now, you see, you've got this fellow scared about himself. Just maybe he can't take a chance on you bluffing him. Now he'll likely try to speak again, but it won't be to get you to leave. He'll likely say he'd like to know what you think he should do about it. Then the rest is up to you. You can string him along about some little job you've got started and how everybody else whose opinions matter are really stirred up about it and how you need a little money to keep it going. Then you're telling him. He isn't sitting there clearing his throat and getting ready to form his lips into a loud 'no'. That's how to get over feeling nervous when you go into a bank." I said that line as if it was the conclusive clincher but the applause was so great that instead of bowing and moving off the stage I hung on for one more glorious moment.

"Well . . . " I dragged it out and basked in the accompanying appreciative applause. "Well . . . when I go into a bank I get nervous. But then what else can be expected from a kid who grew up in a community like this?" Sweeping my arms around in an arc that comprehended the school district I continued in a vein that excited the audience by its unknown possibilities. Even I the speaker had arrived at the point where I was over-extending my good fortune. I didn't want to become insulting and, much less, boring but I simply couldn't shut up.

"Yeah, well . . . what do you expect of a kid that's spent his whole life going to this knock-kneed school and collecting rabbits' hides for war savings certificates in the winter and gopher tails and crow's eggs for bounty payment in the summer? Where's it all getting to anyway?" There was a serious air descending upon the gathering and I was wishing for an easy escape. Why had I added these inconsequential remarks? Anyway folks, that about says the whole thing for all of us. The moral is I guess it's better to be collecting the hides and tails and things than it is to be the rabbit or the gopher or the crow. So in the words of my favorite animal and to save me from arching my back, may I conclude by saying instead of doing, "Bow-wow." A pun is truly cheap humor. For me at this juncture, however, it got me out of a predicament and freed my audience to show they were grateful that a case of stage fright evolved into a new and risky experience for another of the Banner Hall's local youths.

I was so light-headed and ebullient as the laughter and cheers for my monologue rang out, that I forgot that my main job for the night was to work with Albert as stage hands for the main performance of the evening, a play about a girl and her hapless beau. Albert had to come down into the audience to retrieve me from the hugs of my parents and the accolades of relatives and neighbors. Dad was laughing it off with some friends by saying "Always said that kid was a ham. He'll never be a farmer, so might as well let him clown," when Albert yanked me by the arm and said, "C'mon. Mr. Thompson says it's time to set up for the play."

This was the play in which Sally was to be the big star. She had won the part over Joan who was another kid in seventh grade. Sally got the part, Albert and I knew, because she out-maneuvered and outsmarted poor little Joan. Sally had a lot to say when Mr. Thompson was casting the play. She went up to offer to clean a section of the blackboard and we noticed how she worked on Mr. Thompson. Although we both thought Joan said the lines as well as Sally, Sally had ways of making Joan look bad. For example, when she was cleaning the board she was going on to Mr. Thompson about how she was worried about Joan's health since she had the flu because Joan's mother had said to Sally that she hoped Joan wouldn't have too heavy a part in the concert this year. We figured she'd be saying a lot of other sly things like that and knew how it would all come out because Mr. Thompson was such a wonderful person he wouldn't hurt anyone. At least we understood that even if Joan didn't get the part, he'd work in a song or recitation or something for her. There weren't any of us got away without doing something public at the Christmas concert, just like in the singing and speech classes.

Albert and I, therefore, decided it was our duty to even the score for Joan against Sally and make it look like it was God or some higher power who was getting even.

STAGE FRIGHT 79

Maybe that's why God gets blamed for so much badness. There was a place in the play where the young lady hears her boy friend knock on the door and she steps out to greet him, then brings him in by the hand. It was a kind of gummy play where the boyfriend is away fighting a war or something and the girlfriend, Sally, paces around the living room expecting him to arrive back after several years' absence. Most of the words are spoken by this lonesome female who is getting really excited about their reunion. It's supposed to be some town in the Western United States in the winter time.

As she speaks her lines her voice is to show more and more emotion building up to quite a bit of excitement when a train whistle announces the soldier's return. Why she doesn't run to the station we couldn't figure out except maybe it would involve a lot more stage scenery. Anyway her voice get higher and the words come faster as a dog starts to bark. This dog was really Clifford barking off-stage. Then the knock comes and Sally rushes to the door, opens it and runs out into a blinding snowstorm into her boyfriend's arms. The boy's voice and Sally's are then heard as if coming from outside. They don't re-enter the room as the curtains close with them saying nice things to one another in spite of the horrible weather.

The two of us stage hands beside setting up the living room, had to manage the train whistle which we simulated by blowing through a long narrow pipe and we had to knock on the door at the right time and release some white confetti when Sally rushed through the door. This was the snow driving in against her, indicating how strong her love must be for this soldier because she runs right out into it. Albert and I figured that we'd give Sally something to think about besides what a great actress she was and how smart she had been in outwitting Joan in getting the part.

We didn't tell anybody else about it, but we filled a pail full of snow mixed with water which we thought we'd use instead of confetti. We set it against the back door of the hall where the wet snow wouldn't melt. When Sally's voice was getting higher and Clifford started barking, Albert went for the pail while I did the knocking. When the door opened and Sally ran into the back stage area I threw a handful of white confetti through the door onto the stage and Albert dumped the slush over Sally's head. It came off with quite a bang. Sally, who figured she'd really pulled off a great stage performance, ruined her last sentences with a shrieking sound that must have left Mr. Thompson and the others really wondering what was coming off.

Christmas concerts in Banner Hall were fun. It was the crowning event to the old year and an occasion for parents to talk about how well we all did our parts. We got to love and to hate each other more in school during the practises, the rehearsals and performances. And Mr. Thompson became even a greater friend as we got to know him during the trials and foibles of the break in the usual school routine. But I guess the highlight of the whole event was when the program ended, Santa Claus had visited our tree at the front of the hall with its candles actually lit and we all went home with our brown bags of hard candy, an orange and a few nuts. The trip home in a team-driven sleigh box over snow banks and across fields was serene. The muffled voices of the adults brought contentment to us tired kids as we huddled together under a dyed cowhide robe on the straw, our eyes fixed on spaces between stars and our thoughts filled with the joys of school ended and Christmas turkey and toys just ahead.

HAILSTONES AND CHARACTER

Whenever Mother cried it really broke me up. In spite of the insecure feelings her crying caused, however, there was a vindicatory need for me to make her cry some more. It's a strange contradiction but one that illustrates many of the paradoxical facets of human nature. Why does a person dread an unpleasant experience while at the same time setting up the machinery to duplicate the agony? It's my observation that this phenomenon is not so much a personality observation as it is an ego-punishing venture born out of the same psychological root as teasing and bullying.

We were very poor then but we kids didn't know it. Albert's folks were poor too and so were everybody else's. The conditioning was in progress that leads people to value material possessions. Because we had relatively few of these we were taught to respect property. Property was the means by which things got done hence it served basic human needs. Materialism was not one of the spiritual diseases rampant in those days but it was lying dormant until the next generation. People left property unprotected because it wasn't the end of life; it was a means to life and was there to be enjoyed in the community because of its scarcity. Property and goods were scarce but human resources were rich. Co-operatives, Credit Unions and the Wheat Pool were manifestations of this spirit.

It was not unnatural then for a farmer's wife like my mother to wait over long periods of time for some basic equipment like a new motor for the washing machine or even some new wash tubs or dishes or other everyday utensils. She had to know how to conserve and adjust the family needs to the available budget. She learned to sew not as a hobby but because of dire necessity; she cooked delicious meals not because she inherited the instinct but due to the hard facts that a little must be stretched a long way. That was when delicacies such as dandelion leaves and different ways of cooking wild meat were discovered. These taste-teasers found their way to the dining room table because they were available and cheap, not because of some health food fad. The children's clothing were best when they were done-over hand-me-downs. A second or third-hand pair of trousers displayed the mother's genius and creativity with a needle and therefore was worn with pride. Of course, when all your peers are engaged in similar pursuits in similar economic circumstances there's pretty good community spirit about. That's one reason Banner Hall community was such a jumping place.

But sometimes things got so bad that it made Mother cry. In the year that I passed into eighth grade it seemed as if Mom was going to get a few of the things she'd been waiting for. She needed and wanted a new sewing machine and a new cookstove for the kitchen. The repairman in Melville had fixed up the old Singer so often that he despaired each time he saw Mother coming into the shop.

"It's only going to give so many years service, m'am, and then it just can't hold together. I'll give it another try but I really think you should consider my offer on a trade-in. I can give you a dandy that'll work trouble-free for years," he said one day when she came in.

"The way the crop's coming on this year I just may take you up on it, but until then . . . how about this spindle?" Mom was counting on that crop. She'd sell cream and eggs at the Co-op creamery but that would just about cover the flour and sugar and basic foodstuffs not to mention the material required for new clothes and new shoes for two of us kids. Running around barefoot most of the summer was okay but there were Sundays and winter to think about.

And the McClary range had just about had it. The fire box had been repaired so many times with hammered-out tomato tins that it rattled everytime we stuck a stick of wood in the fire. The right back lid had rusted off and it was supported by two bricks on that corner. Mom kept the oven and the surface of the lids shining by rubbing them down with wax paper but the stove was wearing out. She ranked its replacement high on the list of priorities for when the grain was threshed in the fall.

It was a promising year for wheat. Heavy snowfalls in the winter created a voluminous run-off in the spring. The ravines and streams overflowed their shallow banks, causing the sloughs and potholes to fill up to the brim. The water level was higher in the land than usual. Warm, drying winds created a good seedtime and June rains coming on the average of once a week had promoted heavy growth, supporting a long shot blade and the possibility of six-row heads on the wheat. The hay meadows were lush in growth. Prospects were for heavy yields on the summerfallow and abundance of feed for the cattle. Although the wetter than average soil encouraged the possibility of a cutworm outbreak there was little likelihood of the return of the grasshopper menace of the preceding year. The vicissitudes of farming, however, included a number of variables.

Mother ran from window to window whenever a rain cloud appeared. This served two purposes. There was her need to predict the direction and the amount of rainfall. She normally underestimated both of these items. Like anyone whose welfare is dependent upon visible but uncontrolled circumstances and elements there comes a feeling of helplessness and a kind of paranoia which you know is groundless yet somehow it haunts from deep down. Mother would see the cloud coming very close above our fence line even to the point of dropping its shield of water in such a manner that you could follow its direction. Then she would react as if some power above who controlled the system suddenly decided to tease her by pulling the cloud back or changing its direction to let it follow the fence line in a way that let the neighbor's land receive its benefits and passed by ours. We insisted usually that this wasn't the case but she'd remonstrate and say with feeling, "Oh, what's the use. They're getting it over there and we're going to miss it again. Oh, it's maddening." Then it would open up and rain.

Her other need was to check the cloud for the dangerous white and green color denoting hail in the storm. This was a dreadful sight to Mother. When it appeared it was usually in the late afternoon on a hot, humid day while Dad was still out in one of the fields. She had to deal with it alone. Us kids were not much help because in the first place we kind of enjoyed a real storm with lightning, thunder, torrential rain and large hailstones. We liked to go to school the next day and out-boast each other. "They were as large as golf balls at our place" or "Heck, we had some as big as goose eggs" and so on. We knew something of the destructiveness of hail and the loss of crops but we didn't have to make the crucial decisions about what we'd do to survive afterwards. That's what parents were for. Mother had to run from window to window to anticipate whether the storm was a friend or a foe. And by the same mystic insight that told her how the neighbors got most of the rain she was able to foresee how if there was a hail streak in the cloud it would be headed straight for our crops. Having no hail insurance and knowing how good things could be if we got this bumper crop off combined to make my folks very jumpy that summer.

July so far had been unusually hot. The foliage everywhere was responding to the ideal growing conditions. Hay fields and meadows had been cleared of their verdant production and were going in for second growth. The wheat waved various shades of green in the fields as the blossoms were leaving the richly filling heads; oats and barley crops fortokened feed bins full of the stuff that fattens the shorthorns and herefords and helps replenish the milk of Holstein cows. The garden beside the house was beautiful in its potential stock of vegetables for the basement.

A distant flash of lightning streaking down from a huge thunderhead in the west announced the approach of a refreshing summer shower. I was feeding the chickens when I saw it. In a few moments a faraway subdued growl followed as the thunder resounded across the empty sky. The easterly breeze ceased its blowing. A peaceful quiet descended on the entire farm as the huge cloud began to blank out the direct effects of the blistering hot sun. It was so quiet that I could hear Dad's voice a mile away as he guided the six horse outfit from the seat of the cultivator. "C'mon, Trixie, Pat, C'mon; Gee, Haw" and so on. The scraping of the cultivator tooth over a rock seemed to bring him right into the yard. Cows munching grass near the dugout created a soft, tearing sound that added to the aura of peacefulness in the moments before the wind started to pick up again. Mother was hoeing in the garden and she called out,

"Isn't that storm approaching awfully fast?" I watched the amazing configurations of cloud design change as streaks of black folded over its crisp outer edges and striations of light, black and grey wove an interlaced pattern across the centre of the formation which seemed to be the beginning of two clouds melting together. Chain lightning crisscrossed and was intercepted by the bolts of fork lightning slamming prodigious amounts of energy into the ground. The cloud was growing as it approached. Although we were in an area devoid of wind it was obvious there was a massive force pushing the storm towards us. The sound of the thunder now echoed across the fields and bounced from bush to bush. The brightness that had enshrouded us a few minutes earlier was being transformed into a charcoalish effect so that the outlines of the hills and the buildings were becoming hazy as at dusk. The peak of the cloud was arching above us. Now the leaves began a faint rustle, gradually growing in intensity until I could feel the hot rush of moving air brush my cheeks. Dust whipped around in little eddies at several places in the barnyard as if set off by a central signal. The chickens, which had been oblivious of the change while they pecked up the grain I was scattering, began to cackle up a chorus and move towards the chicken house. Mother called,

"We'd better get to the house! Where are the others?" Then as was her custom she raised her bandannad head and cupped her hands over her mouth and ran through the names of my brothers and sisters she knew to be in the vicinity at the time. We ran to the house even as the wind whipped the iron gate on the yard fence back and forth and sent some spilled straw swirling over our heads.

Mother started the pre-storm ritual.

"Close those upstairs windows. Shut the front door. Let that darned dog in." Jet was scratching at the back door which we'd closed as the last one arrived. She went to the west window and said, "That's a mean one coming. Wonder if it'll get time to drop any rain or will it just blow on by?" Then she scurried through the dining room and turned right to get a view to the south of us.

"Look at that! Kosha's are going to get it the heaviest again. Just look at that dust cloud. And wow! see that lightning." We all interchanged stations at the various windows. Some upstairs and some down. Giggling and pushing and complaining about the others' elbows, we jockeyed for the best spots; hoping to catch sight of the mightiest lightning flash and see the first huge splats of water as the rain blotted into the dust. "Oh dear, look at that ugly white strip!" Her voice sounded ominous. Near the core of the cloud, masses of black and blue cascaded over and over creating a waterfall effect. Just below this marvelous cyclorama a definite outline of a peculiar characteristic of such storms coalescing on hot, humid days was taking its portentous shape. A greenish, yellow streak was rapidly descending. Near the point of this phenomenon its edges were well-defined but irregular. At its base point a whitish purple indicated its depth and abundant resources. It was the dreaded hail strip. It might be a half mile or more wide. If it came down it would dump its ravaging load mercilessly on the greenery and the buildings and strive to wipe out as much as nature would allow.

Enormous drops of water bounced off the roof of the back porch. A darkened room and a blinding flash of light proclaimed the cloud opening upon us. Torrents of water slid down the west side of our house as the gale force winds ripped through the cloud's centre. Little troughs along the garden path filled up and overflowed, the lawn became a shimmering lake in a few minutes. Mother went into the back porch. I followed her because I knew I couldn't get hurt by her side. Her face showed a strain that wasn't there earlier. Before I could ask her what was wrong, nature itself announced it.

The roof above us began to bang and crackle as the first hailstones came down. Hailstones falling without a wind pushing them do not carry the devastation that these carried. The wind smashed them into the ground and rolled them across its surface. Lightning seemed to originate all around us in the west, the east, the north and south. One crack of thunder roared into the next as the sky unleashed a fury of recrimination as savage as a giant gone mad. What a sharp contrast to the stifling calm preceding this galloping storm!

"Oh my God, please, no, don't let it!" mother was calling as if the storm had ears. And as if in arrogant answer to a helpless plea it responded with more wind, more velocity and noise. The hail cascaded down. "Merciful Lord, no; don't let it happen. Think of the children, the long winter. O God, no!" mother repeated as if to challenge the whole existence. It seemed so futile. So lonely. The ground was covered now with varied chunks and shapes of ice, the smaller pieces whirling around in the little rivulets and pools, the larger ones stuck in ugly patterns across the ground. The wind raged on and more ice-spiked rain hurtled down. My Mother now was quiet but troubled-looking. She didn't go back into the house, she just stared despairingly out the door of that back kitchen as we sometimes called it.

In a few moments it was all over. An icy chill surrounded us. It was quiet again except for the gurgling sounds of the hundreds of little rivers created by the preceding outbreak.

"Mom, look at those stones!" I shouted as I ran in bare feet to retrieve some of the icy giants. She didn't seem to hear me as she passed by me and went out the gate towards the wheat field back of the barn where one of our best stands of wheat was growing. It was in that direction that Dad would be coming home. I followed a short distance behind her. I sensed somehow that this was going to be a very bad moment.

She seemed taller as she walked erectly towards the gate of the field. It was set between two poplar bluffs. She was beautiful as she walked ahead of me. There was an air of grace and elegance about her which I felt as she moved some distance ahead of me. What she was thinking or where she was going I couldn't be sure. She walked with a sense of purpose and direction. I recall wondering why she suddenly appeared to be lighter than before. Her feet hardly made prints in the mud. With her head held high she adeptly dropped the barbed wire gate and walked part way into the field. I stopped in my tracks. The beautiful flowing waves of wheat had been smashed and broken into the soil. Even the lumps of dirt and stones showed above the demolished plants. It was all over.

Mother stood there for a long while. I didn't know what to do or what to say. I stuck to my tracks and felt terribly upset. She just stood there looking across the field with her elbows arched out and her hands on her hips. Then after what seemed to me to be a long time, she turned slightly towards me but didn't see me. Her body wilted a little from its beautiful poise and she walked slowly and resolutely over to a large poplar tree. Forgetting where she was and who she was she looped her arms around that tree and sort of hung to one side letting her head rest against the tree's trunk. Her body started to shake and quiver. Then I could hear her cry. I felt terrible. I had to look back towards the house. Then I turned to face her again when

I heard another voice. Dad had come to her and he had both his arms around her. I heard him say,

"There, there, it's going to be all right, Beckie, don't cry." That was a name I guess he used for her when they were young lovers. He used that name often when he thought we kids wouldn't hear. I knew that he was using it now because he knew how hard thing really were for Mom and for all of us. There would be no new sewing machine; no new stove.

I repeat a question I started with. Why does a person dread an unpleasant experience like this while at the same time setting off the machinery to duplicate the agony?

As it turned out, our crop was a hundred percent loss on the half section near the house including, of course, the quarter on which the homestead was located. Only a small portion of the wheat and oats had been struck by this storm on land we owned a half mile north of the house. This was some consolation as it meant that unless another storm hit prior to harvest, the heavy rain accompanying this storm would assure a fairly heavy yield in that half section.

One hot afternoon several days later another less vicious looking storm appeared from the southwest. Mother was in the back kitchen preserving saskatoon berries. She had a tub of water boiling on the old cookstove and couldn't leave it to take up her lookout positions in the house. There were streaks of lightning and rumbles of thunder but not of the threatening quality of the ruinous storm that visited our place earlier.

"How does it look?" she called out to me.

"I think it looks bad, Mom!" I shouted in return from the top of the little hill in the backyard. Actually I knew I was exaggerating and I was aware that Mother could not join me or verify my reports at this juncture. But I persisted in perpetrating one of the foulest kinds of fabrication. One couldn't classify this as teasing; it was juvenile maliciousness.

Thunder growled closer and closer. The trees around the house began their ritual dance. There would be a nice summer shower but not a dangerous storm. I was certain of this but I continued my embellished deceptiveness. Moving nearer to the house I called out,

"There's a nasty white and green streak heading right over us." Just as I said this some large drops of rain started to fall and the wind picked up a little.

"Oh, Mom, here it comes," I shouted. To my disgust and shame I must report

HAILSTONES AND CHARACTER

that I had picked up a handful of small stones and started casting them, singly, then two and three at a time, on the shingled roof above my Mother's head. The rain began to fall in a fairly heavy shower. The combined effects of the stones rolling off the roof and the gentle rain that was falling caused my Mother to drop whatever she was doing and rush to the door. I was caught in the act performing a deed that has never brought much satisfaction to my memory of that particular day.

We are born with the potential of being either very loving or becoming very cruel. Along the way we decide which it will be for us. Fortunate are the children who recognize these latent powers early enough to be able to isolate the alternatives. Of course, good mothers and fathers help.

HIRAM THE HIRED MAN

Hiram Jackson was a special breed of man. He was a hired man and a keen student of human relations. These two characteristics combined to make Hiram one of Banner Hall's great guys. He was sought after on social occasions because of his willingness to be the brunt of many jokes and his ability to tap dance. Hiram had been shell shocked in the First World War, which rendered him incapable of functioning fully on his own. The results of this psychological condition was that he needed someone around him who could make decisions for him, that is, decisions that affected his ultimate welfare — like knowing how to plan for his own needs. He required close supervision when he worked, or he'd get into all sorts of jams. He acted like he couldn't see straight sometimes, for example.

One day I saw him driving a team-drawn hay rack between two buildings that in no way left a wide enough space for the vehicle. The horses got scared when the rack got stuck and they jumped ahead pulling the wheel's portion of the wagon out from under the rack and leaving poor Hiram stranded against the boards trying to pull the reins and hold the horses back. The horses kept going and Hiram hung on. The reins were strong, Hiram was stubborn, but the horses were stronger so Hiram got pulled right over the end of the rack and onto the ground. He was dragged along beside the wheels of the wagon until he got the team stopped. Then he had to go and get help and accept the bawling out that went with this error in judgement. Although he was a big man he always accepted these reprimands with the passivity of a scolded child.

On Saturday nights when Dad was cutting us kids' hair outside the back kitchen, sometimes Charlie Zentyas would come along with his fiddle. While the hair was flying and the conversation started to wane, Charlie would start a little tune on the fiddle. During the two years that Hiram worked at our place we could count on this fiddle music drawing him out of the old granary which had been pulled into the yard for his summer bunkhouse and coming over to dance a little jig or do a tap dance for our entertainment.

It was always quite a sight for us kids. Hiram must have weighed all of 225 pounds. He'd hitch up the pants of his coveralls exposing the full length of his old army boots with their thick soles and had let loose on the boards of the walk leading up to the back step. Charlie would start slow enough on the fiddle, sort of enticing Hiram to pick up the beat; then when his giant feet started their shuffle hop step and the boards started to groan, the tempo would increase and Hiram sort of lost control of his body, that is, he couldn't always keep in step when the music got faster but instead of dropping out he'd stay with it until the music stopped. It was kind of a cruel sport which we all enjoyed thoroughly and Hiram appeared to appreciate the fact we were being entertained. Actually his love for people and his special insight into what motivated people kept him in the business of bringing this kind of vicarious pleasure to all of us. He was able to hide any hurt feelings he had as well as keep disguised the special understandings he had about why people acted this way.

Albert and I became appreciative of Hiram's sterling qualities at a dance at Banner Hall. We got to understand just how well this great man was able to take other people's cruelty into himself and not fight back actively. His method was to absorb the hurt and let circumstances work themselves out. I don't think many other people ever understood this.

Because fiddle music attracted Hiram like a dish of milk lured cats from the barn, some of the local guys thought it would be a great joke to get Hiram into the dance hall and perform for the crowd as a highlight to the evening's entertainment. Hiram wasn't a drinker because of the way liquor acted on his poor frightened brain so they knew it was useless to ply him with homebrew to improve the act. This did not, however, discourage these fellows from treating themselves first and adding Hiram's share to their own to fortify their courage whilst introducing the comedy act for the night. The normally soft-spoken Mac got loud; Cecil's quiet unassuming manner became aggressive and cutting; Jack's normally phlegmatic personality took on some startling new qualities of excitement and stimulation. The brew set fire to latent powers that didn't really enhance their images.

The trio conspired with the orchestra. We noticed Mac sort of bounce right up on the stage on the last steps of a polka. He let his partner go on a whirl and gave a kind of "whoop" as he leapt. The other two chaps entered the stage from the side door. The orchestra leader motioned to the fiddle player to come forward and join their little huddle. In a moment or two he was nodding his head as if he was listening to some plan and understanding it as it unravelled. Then one of the boys reached into his pocket and took out a bill and handed it to the fiddler. The three of them returned to the main floor laughing loudly and looking pleased as three little boys with new toys. It was obvious that some diabolical plan was about to make its auspicious beginning.

Hiram was outside the front door of the hall talking quietly to people as they arrived and passed him on their way into the dance.

"Hi, Hiram!" they called, "how's tricks at the farm? Been to any good wars lately?" It was cruel in content but good-natured in delivery for the most part. When young men enter places of entertainment with their girl friends they normally release some tension and try to sound witty in this way. Hiram's condition was well-known around the community. Prior to the war he'd been a pretty sharp individual and if he'd come out of it with all of his faculties in order he no doubt would have ended up in a managerial position in some business. The part that we liked about him still was there fortunately. We knew that he had a special concern for kids and because of this he saw more deeply into most adults too than these same adults gave him credit for. Now because of his dependence on kind farmers like my Dad for his livelihood and his demands on their patience for the necessary concentrated kind of understanding, he couldn't last more than a year or so on any one farm. I consider that my Dad's kindness and patience outmeasured that of many of our neighbors' in that he gave this energy-sapping assistance for two full years. By this time Hiram had stayed with and worked for three quarters of the farmers in the area so almost everyone knew him personally.

When the music stopped after the polka and the three chaps finished whatever they were talking about with the orchestra, the dancers sensed that there was going to be a hiatus in the round of waltzes, foxtrots and polkas in which some special announcement or an act would be introduced. Everyone moved into corners and conversed in small groups or sat down on the benches that lined the walls. Some people began to look expectantly at the trio who moved into the centre of the circle. Cecil raised his hand and the drummer rendered a flourish on the snare drums. Jack bowed in a waggish gesture towards Mac who slipped his right hand into his jacket in a Napoleonic stance and raised his head as if to prepare for the delivery of an important speech.

"Ladies and gentlemen," he began. The little groups stopped buzzing, and those standing turned in the direction of Mac's voice. Those sitting craned their necks to peer around any standing in front of them. All listened in mock attentiveness knowing that whatever announcement was to follow would be the introduction to some enjoyable devilry as was the case when these three plotted together. The crowd was in a mood of anticipative alertness, prepared to enjoy whatever was to follow.

Having enticed his audience to this psychological mood of expectancy, Mac continued.

"Your small committee of three stalwarts," he touched each other man on the arm and pointed to himself. This brought a unanimous roar of approval from the audience and a hearty clapping of hands, "this usually hardworking trio who think not of themselves but only of your pleasure has come up with the crowning act of the evening. We know you will want to thank us for our consideration of you. You have already expressed this thanks in the usual manner. Perhaps as the program unwinds you will find it in your hearts to express your feelings with a bit more shall we say tangible means. That may be too big a word for some of you, but just look into your hearts and follow the example of others and you'll know what I mean."

"Yeah, follow the leader!" interjected Jack.

"Please," Mac pretended to rebuke this interruption as he raised his forefinger to Jack's lips. "In a few moments I'm going to invite our violinist," he put considerable emphasis on this term realizing that we normally referred to him as a fiddler, "to commence playing a round of jigs and rather fast-moving music to which tap dancing can be performed. You will be pleased to note that we have imported from far afield some talent unequalled in quality in this particular community which as you all know is rather well-blessed with gifts. We've had to search widely for this performer. He has travelled around the world." In a flurry of words denoting very bad taste which was pulled off because of the psychologically willing audience he referred to the performer's work amongst troops in the battle fields. The crowd would howl with delight later when they realized that Hiram's battle shock experience was being alluded to.

"Now, dear friends," Mac was so enjoying his little speech and its effect upon the audience that he switched to a kind preacher-like pulpit tone, "my very dear friends, and gathered loved ones, I invite your full attention to a few details which we all must co-operate in if we are to bring this performer inside the hall. You see, although we have managed through our hard work and much expenditure of personal funds to bring him this far, he is reluctant to face such an important audience. He is not sure that you will really appreciate him so he has decided to await your public invitation. Ladies and gentlemen, outside that door stands a great tapdancer, world-renowned but a bit shy of this particular crowd." Mac faced the door. "Are we going to let this star think we are unappreciative? If we call out his name and clap our hands like this," the three demonstrated a spaced clapping of their hands, "and call out like this, 'Hiram, come and dance for us!' I think perhaps he will condescend. Let's give it the old Banner Hall try."

The crowd clapped and some men whistled and everyone seemed caught up in the spirit of the performance so far. Albert and I probably showed as much enthusiasm as the others on our faces, but we moved elbow to elbow and exchanged a couple of glances that revealed to each other how we really felt inside. We were not happy about the turn of events. We knew that Hiram was just outside that door and that up 'til now in his own rather innocent way he was enjoying himself as people passed by and he was able to call most of them by name. We knew he wouldn't cause anyone any trouble and we also knew that in his childlike mind he would be naive enough to get sucked in on whatever plan these villains had conspired to enact. But we didn't know how to cope with these kinds of feelings so we kept on laughing when everybody laughed and we clapped with everybody else.

Mac waved his hand at the orchestra. Once again the drummer rolled out an introduction. The fiddler started in on turkey in the straw. Feet began stomping and hands commenced to clap rhythmically. The trio started their chant. Other voices soon echoed the call:

"Hiram Jackson come and dance! Hiram, Hiram now's your chance!"

The hall literally bounced to the beat of the stamping feet, the fiddler's inspired enthusiasm and rollicking rhythm and the pulsation of the clapping hands in time with the measured chorus of voices:

"Hiram Jackson come and dance! Hiram, Hiram now's your chance!"

Albert and I caught up in the psychodramatic crowd added our high-pitched voices to the others. We knew that through that door, which we all faced, in a moment or two would come a kind of shy-looking but taken Hiram. He would run awkwardly to the centre of the floor and his large feet would begin to respond to the beat of the music. We didn't wait long. The door opened and a shaft of light pierced the summer night's darkness through which walked the star of the floor show. He was pathetic in his innocence, letting a big, lazy grin break across his rather flabby face. His large puffy hands were already designing little arcs in the air as he bounced heavily across the dance floor. The crowd's syncopated clapping broke into a massive swell of constant applause. Some cheers went up. Then the people who had stood up to welcome their guest, resumed their seated positions and leaned back against the wall in a relaxed attitude of spectator enjoyment.

"Let'er go, Hiram. Ladies and gentlemen, I give you Hiram Jackson, tap dancer of no small renown!" Mac shouted as he waved up the music of the fiddler. Hiram basked in the round of applause and his massive body turned and whirled freely as his giant boots beat down on the floor a tapdance in the style of his Prince Edward Island forbears.

The fiddler whirled through several stanzas of "turkey in the straw" and without so much as a pause broke into the more rapid paces of "the Irish washerwoman"; the crowd liked that and showed its approval by toe-tapping and resuming its rhythmic clapping. The trio who started the whole thing had broken their ranks and moved to various parts of the assembly. They knelt down at the front of the lines of people and beat their hands furiously in time with the music. Then coins began to appear on the dance floor. Albert and I heard the first clink and thinking that someone had dropped a coin we were about to rush and pick it up in the community-honored tradition of "Finders keepers, losers weepers" when we realized that Jack and Cecil and Mac were consciously digging into their pockets and digging out dimes, pennies and nickels and were tossing them into the midst of the circle near Hiram's fast-moving feet. This in turn incited others to emulate the practice. We knew that these three were now encouraging the payoff to which they had indirectly referred earlier.

The crowd was moving into a high-pitched state of nearly hysterical euphoria. The fiddler switched adeptly from one tune to another and poor Hiram was showing signs of tiring out. Sweat ran down his face; his hair flung carelessly in all directions and his armpits spilled fluid into his shirt so that long dark streaks spread out like a spider web, staining as it moved.

The two of us who had been caught up in the mob psychology now looked at each other again and were reminded of what we really felt for our friend who was being tortured before our very eyes. And we were enjoying his sacrifice. Almost as if we had verbalized these thoughts, we moved back into a corner and tore ourselves free of the grip of the cruel crowd. Hiram could not break the spell that this kind of music cast over his troubled mind. He was the victim of that group and only a break in the music or some other kind of intervention would free him.

"Quick, let's get outside," I motioned to Albert. We ran across the back of the hall and stepped into the refreshing air.

"They're going to kill old Hiram," Albert protested. "What're we going to do?"

The resounding clapping and the din of bouncing feet greeted our ears as the two of us huddled close to the step. The fiddler, recognizing Hiram's growing weariness, slowed the tempo somewhat but did not break the trance he held over his duped prey. The sound of coins rolling across the floor continued while shouts of "C'mon Hiram, keep those feet moving!" and "Hey, hey, don't give up now!" resounded from the building. The stream of light stretched across the bushes and danced in time with the music. The window frames wiggled and bent against the edges between light and dark.

"Mr. Thompson is not in there tonight or that nonsense wouldn't be going on," Albert observed.

"Hey, yes, that's it!" I cried, pulling Albert away from the step. "Let's get over there fast. To the teacherage. Let's go get Mr. Thompson to phone Dad. He'll get over here real fast and do something. C'mon, Albert for gosh sake," I hollered impatiently even as Albert began to outrun me up the path through the inky dark bushes, by the old school barn, on up the hill to the school and teacherage. The Thompsons' light was still on, cutting a nice swath through the darkness for us as we ran up onto the step. Even before we hit the door with our knuckles, Mr. Thompson opened it and said,

"What're you two up to? Looks like you're being chased. What's the matter?"

Between puffs and interchanged corrections we told the story and asked to use the phone.

"Yes, quickly, use the phone," he said, looking troubled, and picking up his jacket which was draped over a kitchen chair.

I cranked out the required three long and two shorts on the party line and waited for my Dad's voice. When Mom answered, all I said was, "Mom, hurry, tell Dad Hiram's in trouble at the dance and we need him right away." Mom tried in vain to get more information, but I disappointed her inquiries by saying, "Mr. Thompson's going over. Albert and I, we've got to go along. Tell Dad to hurry." I hung up.

Mr. Thompson had difficulty in keeping up with the two of us who at this point had no idea of what we were going to do when we got back to the hall. We ran back through the bush on the west side of the hall and waited for him to catch up with us.

The music was still pouring out. We could hear the crowd yelling the same kind of encouraging calls to Hiram, but the pace had decreased noticeably in the short time we'd been away. Mr. Thompson caught up. He ran up the steps and swung the door open loud enough for some of the enrapt persons near the door to notice his entry. Palms sweating and cheeks flushed from their involvement, they broke from the proceedings long enough to size up how truly involved they were in the enjoyment of Hiram's indignity. They straightened up a bit at Mr. Thompson's entry and quietened a little.

"Stop it! Stop this foul joke in the name of humanity! Have you all lost your minds?" Mr. Thompson shouted. The fiddler didn't seem to notice and the music went on. Hiram, who was by now haggard and drawn, his clothing soaked in perspiration, heard the voice but continued his exhausted dance even as he half-smiled towards Mr. Thompson's gesture.

"My God, in the name of decency can't you people see what you're doing?" Mr. Thompson burst through the lines of people and half-tripped over the coins spilled loosely around the place where Hiram danced.

He could see that Hiram would keep on somehow as long as the fiddler kept playing. That man now looked slightly worried as he noticed this intrusion into the evening's fun for which he had been monetarily rewarded in advance. Mr. Thompson ran up to the stage where the orchestra sat and commanded the fiddler to desist. The music stopped. Someone shouted out "Killjoy!" and several "Boos" followed. Mr. Thompson was about to speak again, but was interrupted by Hiram who although completely wilted by this inhuman one man marathon tap dance, broke into a weird sort of hop, skip and jump and shouted out something garbled that sounded like, "I can't help myself; I had to do it; they need this kind of torture or they'll kill others; they got to rid themselves of this need to kill..." It probably wasn't just that he said; he spoke so haltingly at the best of times, but both Albert and I knew that he could see into the hearts and minds of his tormentors. Mr. Thompson was approaching Hiram, but Hiram's attempt to verbalize whatever it was he was trying to get across was too much for him. He began to sob and stammer out something, while staggering towards the door. He burst into the night. Several of the hissing, booing young men followed. These men didn't like Mr. Thompson's intrusion and they were showing him so by pursuing poor old Hiram. We noticed, however, that several others sat down again and looked rather bothered about what had just taken place. Most of the women in fact looked quite ashamed. Some of the men ran over to talk with Mr. Thompson like kids who've been caught doing mischief and who want to be the first to own up to the fact that what was happening was beyond their control.

"It was Mac and Jack and Cecil, over there," some of these fellows exclaimed. These three, incidentally, were intent on scraping up into little piles the scattered coins. These they collected into a little cloth bag.

Outside the hall, the pursuers of Hiram shouted taunts and jeers at him wherever he was hiding. Albert and I wanted to be close to him but we feared these men who had now become hunters encircling a scared rabbit. Hiram had to be close at hand because they went after him so quickly. He must be hiding in the bushes or behind a car. The men organized their chase into a sweep of the yard. Then it happened. A lonely, desolate scream cut through the hushed night. One of the men discovered Hiram, shaking, frightened and worn out, crying in the darker shadows of a parked car. The man had kicked him in the rear end as he provoked Hiram's voice to that scream.

"Here he is! Come and get him!" this chap called out as easily as he might call a threshing gang to dinner. The others began to run in his direction. Some of them had had so much to drink that they stumbled and tripped over mounds of grass as they moved gleefully in the direction of the voice. Albert and I felt a deep regret sweep through the pits of our stomachs. What would they do? A couple of guys pulled Hiram to his feet. Another let go a fist into his ribs. Wildly crying into the night Hiram's voice attracted the attention of Mr. Thompson and some of the newly turned sympathizers and shamed hunters of a few moments before. They moved towards the small group of bitter, semi-crazed men.

A car was roaring up the road from the east. Its motor was responding to its driver's anxiety. It began to slow as the Banner Hall gates were outlined by the headlights. Squealing brakes brought it to a skidding halt as it turned into the yard; the motor was left on as the driver door flung open and my Dad jumped to the ground.

"What's the matter here?" his voice boomed through the night. The whimpering sounds of Hiram were the only other utterances heard maybe fifteen yards from where Dad stood. Mr. Thompson had already run across to Hiram's side and the misdemeanants shrunk back into the shadows expecting more trouble than they could cope with at the moment.

"Over here, Dad," I hollered, moving out from the protective shroud of darkness now that I felt safe and wanting to follow through on the rescue that Albert and I had begun earlier.

Dad ran over to Mr. Thompson's side. Poor old Hiram, feeling the presence of friends, prostrated his hurting body at the feet of these two tall men. He cried unrestrainedly and put his arms around my Dad's legs.

"Those guys, they don't understand it all," he blubbered. "Don't hurt them or blame them; they're not mean men, only they have so much stuff inside they got to get out. Hiram won't hurt long. It's okay with Hiram."

Dad and Mr. Thompson with the tenderness they might use in lifting a baby from the ground, lifted Hiram up on to his feet. With their arms around him they supported him and moved towards the car with the open door.

"Okay, Hiram, we'll try to forget what they did to you. But God help them if they ever try something like this to you or anyone else ever again." My Dad's voice had that forgiving firmness that contained the unmistakeable marks of principle combined with readiness that great men's voices show.

THE EYE OF GOD AND THE VANILLA BOTTLE

I'm not sure where we first heard that some people regularly got high on vanilla. I do remember how the idea intrigued us though. Albert and I used to talk about it at recess quite a bit when the other kids were off doing something else. There are some subjects that you discuss best in the confines of a certain security and this was one of them. The whole school paired off for hide and seek, using the entire confines of the Runneberg yard and the Banner Hall yard. Albert and I crouched near the fence line in the south willow trees.

"I hear Alfred and Antosio were found in a wagon box at the school barn after the dance last Friday," said Albert, "drunker'n a couple of skunks. Her dad found vanilla bottles under the straw."

"What'd he do to them?" I asked, hoping for a pretty juicy bit of gossip.

"Well, first he pulled Alfred off onto the ground and roughed him up a bit; then he grabbed Antosio and really shook her. Said if he ever caught her drinking and sleeping around with the likes of Alfred again she'd be walking out of this community with a tanned hide and a broken leg. Said he couldn't understand why kids would horse around with things like liquor and sex, then he picked up the vanilla bottles and heaved them into the bush farther than a professional baseball player could hit a ball, he was so mad. He said that vanilla was what Indians and drunkards took because they were too stupid and stoned to know any better. Then he walked off leaving the two of them really shamefaced and bleary-eyed. Frank was telling me that he saw it all since he was hiding in the barn at the time."

"Yeah, and if I know Frank it's because he had vanilla hid in one of the mangers," we were getting worldy-wise as our eighth grade year was coming to a close.

We scrunched down into the long grass surrounding the willow trees. The team that was "it" was getting close to us. They walked within five yards of where we were lying and missed us. Having a few more moments to pursue the subject which we both found fascinating I picked up on it with,

"Wonder what it's like?"

"What's what like?" asked Albert acting stupid.

"You know, getting stuff like vanilla inside of you and acting goofy and that sort of thing. Wonder what it's like?"

"Dad says that drinking vanilla and alcohol from the shop or that sort of thing will make you blind and kill you if you take enough of it." Albert's dad was the community's best carpenter and he knew about all kinds of fluids and things". I think our dads say things like that about that kind of stuff because they're afraid we'll try it sometime and find out it's not as bad as they make it out to be," I said provocatively. Albert picked up on this being of a similar bent of mind as myself

"Yeah, that's true. If those two drank a couple of bottles of the stuff and were still around to be shook up by her dad in the morning, it's likely it didn't do them any harm. Maybe vanilla hasn't got the high class of homebrew or scotch but it's likely okay for cheap parties. I'll bet if guys wanted to just on their own they could have a a darned good time drinking the stuff. We were getting to where either of us could easily make the proposition without turning the other off.

"Okay," said Albert, "let's sometime get us a bottle of vanilla and see for ourselves." "Okay," I said as we both got up and brushed the grass and twigs off our clothes as the school bell rang the end of recess.

Once we had verbalized our mutual desire to try the stuff, it was easy to talk about our expectations of what the vanilla might do to us. What was not so easy however, was to actually go and purchase the bottle of vanilla. In the first place if we decided to buy it during one of the trips with our parents to Melville there was the danger of being seen with this one grocery item and being asked what it was for. We decided it was too risky to buy it in town since most of our trips involved someone else from the family.

Another option was to go three miles east of where we lived to the little village of McKim. There were three elevators and one little general store there. The problem here, however, was to make the purchase of one bottle of vanilla and to act as if that was just what one of our mothers needed to complete some baking job underway in her kitchen. We were so well-known at this community store that we knew we couldn't just go up to the counter and ask for a bottle of vanilla. The friendly storekeeper and his wife would both be there. They'd want to know all about the family, what everybody was doing and how come Mother forgot to buy vanilla the last time she came for groceries.

Our mothers were so well-organized in this department that it was practically impossible for them to forget an important item like this if they were low on it. Of course, we could say that they usually bought vanilla from the Rawleigh's man or the Watkin's man and that he hadn't come for quite a spell. But then this sort of conversation would land us into the dilemma of someday soon having to explain the story before our mothers when the Watkin's or the Rawleigh's man came next time since he'd have heard of our purchase at the store in the name of one of our mothers. If we went straight up to the counter and asked for vanilla, they'd be certain to ask what mother was baking. Such a dilemma. We knew what we wanted to do but we couldn't structure the situation in such a way that we'd be above suspicion.

After discussing the pros and cons of purchasing the bottle of vanilla in a store and using quite a large percentage of our hard-earned allowance in doing so, we gave up that particular method. Instead we'd get an empty bottle each and pilfer small amounts of the flavoring extract from our mothers' pantries. We decided one day after school that we'd have to do this over a week or two so that our moms would think the bottle was going down due only to their excessive cooking habits of late. Eventually they'd buy some more and we'd borrow a little more and no-one would notice.

"It's a good idea anyway," said Albert, "because we won't be spending our money on something foolish." That sounded like a weak argument but I agreed heartily.

"That's right. Our folks would really be upset if they thought we were spending our money on junk that makes Indians drunk. This way we won't actually be stealing, or hurting anybody else." I had heard my Father say that people's habits weren't bad as long as they didn't get in the way of another person's rights or happiness.

We each got a small bottle with a screw cap on it. The one I used was a large size aspirin bottle. Albert got himself what I think was an old medicine bottle. We washed them out well and prepared for the initial filching. We would use our own resources and ingenuity in carrying out this sensitive portion of the operation. Boy, it's hard to commit robbery when all your conditioning has set you against it. It's easy to imagine that you'd like to purloin and burglarize but actually carrying it through is another thing. Some of this was undoubtedly due to the large family Bible that sat on the end table near our chesterfield.

In this massive black book with heavy leather and cardboard binding in the space between the Old Testament and the New Testament were several pages for family memoirs. There was a spot for birth certificates, my folks' marriage certificate and some pages set out with details of our family tree. The dates of special happenings like Baptisms and other weddings within the family were also recorded. At the end of this section of memorabilia and just before the first page of the Gospel according to Matthew was a page devoted to the eye of God. This was a terrifying picture to a child. It was likely intended by the artist to be a loving reminder of the omnipresence of God. To me it was a constant reminder that there was nothing that was left unknown about me to the giant-size person above us who watched everything I did. Maybe he wasn't wise enough to know or understand what I was thinking about, but his eye bugged out at me every time I actually carried through something I may have thought about for some time.

This eye of God haunted me very early in my childhood and would continue to more or less haunt my actions for several years. On one occasion shortly after I started school I came home as usual very hungry. One treat that mother often prepared for us but which we mustn't do ourselves because of the market value of those products in hard times was a mixture of very thick cream and fresh honey. Since the thickest cream always coalesced at the top of the cream can I decided to fix my own treat this one time in spite of mother's warning that she was taking all the cream into the creamery and we couldn't have our extra treat. I waited for everyone to get on with their outside chores, then I slipped down the basement stairs to the cream can storage area. Prying off the lid I scooped a half cupful of absolutely rich thick covering into a dish. Then back up to the kitchen I scampered and to the cupboard where I'd find a can of fresh honey. All mine. But then that terrifying image appeared in my mind. The eye of God seemed to literally leap from the closed book and hover over me. There was no way I could enjoy that dish. Before I could mix a spoonful of honey with the cream, I dropped the spoon into the drawer and dashed back downstairs. With deftness I pried off the lid again and slid the caseated dense stuff back into the can. Then back upstairs to clean the plate in case the evidence might be misinterpreted. Then, casting a disdainful glance at the imaginary eye above me, I ran outside to do my chores.

Now the eye of God would once again stand sentinel over my actions. Now that I was near the conclusion of my eighth grade and had a much more sophisticated view about such primitve beliefs, still the more recent abstract thinking that was shoving aside the literalistic picture images did not by any means lose its effect. Figuratively speaking or not, the eye of God was somehow present causing me to evaluate my actions and bring some kind of judgement on me for acting contrary to my verbalized beliefs.

I could not let Albert get ahead of me though. This helped to counter my inner

THE EYE OF GOD AND THE VANILLA BOTTLE

religious convictions a little, but not enough to motivate slick action. After school one day I waited for mother to start milking the cows. Once she began this chore there was very little likelihood that she'd come back into the house. The other kids were about the yard at different tasks. I brought in my little bottle which had been hidden under some leaf mold behind the outside toilet. I got the vanilla bottle down off the pantry shelf. My hands began to shake as I removed the lid. What was going on anyway? I murmured something like "Eye of God, go and do something worthwhile for a change." My hands steadied enough to allow a bit of the liquid to run from the main bottle to my sampler. Some of it ran along the rim and down the side. I wiped it off with my finger, which became stained from the vanilla. With relief I replaced the caps and the bottles to their storage places. Now I had to clean the smell of vanilla off my hands. I started thinking how stupid crime really was if it made you feel so miserable inside.

The next day at school I felt better when I checked with Albert and found that he hadn't started on his supply. He said it was hard to find a time when everybody was out of the house, so I thought to myself that he was having a similar problem with his eye of God. I figured with his Roman Catholic background he'd be having an even more miserable time because he'd have to go to Confession and would feel doubly guilty when he couldn't tell the priest what he'd been doing. That was one great advantage of being Protestant, you could let on you were telling all about your life in a direct conversation with God during the minister's long prayer on Sunday. Albert and the others like him had to break up their religious lives into little sections and couldn't enjoy the more mystic and philosophical accoutrements of Protestants. Ours really seemed like a more civilized form of faith.

The next time I retrieved my bottle and made the exchange of fluid from the larger bottle to the smaller my hand didn't quiver quite as much. I didn't have to worry on this round about spilled vanilla and aromatic hands. The time after that and the time after that went easier still. I was getting a fair volume of liquid in my treasure bottle. In the meantime Albert was having some success in his mother's pantry. One day at school we decided it was time to act decisively on the testing arrangements. My mother had purchased another bottle of vanilla not having said anything about the rather rapid diminishing of her supply. This bottle having gone down also rather rapidly, I assumed I'd be pushing my luck if I tried for much more. Albert affirmed similar feelings.

"Where'll we demolish the stuff?" Albert asked. "We could try it some day right here after all the others have gone."

"The problem with that, Albert, is that supposing we do get sort of shook up and stinko, you know like we've seen Gus with his medicine or some of those other guys. It'd be too late in the day to straighten out before chores. We better think of some other way."

"How about telling Mr. Thompson some day that we've got to go home and work in the fields after recess in the afternoon?" he suggested. "The older guys have used that trick a couple of times for whatever they do."

"Yeah," I said, but feeling guilty already, continued, "but we'd have to tell a lie to Mr. Thompson. I hate doing anything like that to him. Also, he might just check on us. No, I don't go for that at all."

"Okay, you come up with the idea then. I'm trying for heaven's sake! Why don't you come up with something I can pee on." Albert never was much for searching for reconciliatory terminology when he got pushed.

"Well, for a starter how about waiting for a Saturday or Sunday. We could take off on some joint effort or other and have the better part of a day to experiment. There's a picnic at Banner Hall next week. We could get ourselves lost for awhile." I caught a little enthusiasm for my own suggestion and felt a bit superior to Albert for the moment. He couldn't respond with eagerness immediately because of my putting down his ideas.

"Picnics are for other things. You know how much chasing around and exploring we always do. Besides we'll likely be playing ball at this one." We had grown taller through the winter and were being touted by some of the Banner Hall team as possible recruits in the new season.

I had to follow through a little more. "Maybe we could bring our bottles to the picnic and if we didn't get picked to play we might use some of our time on this special project."

"Yeah, maybe we could consider doing that," Albert conceded. I figured he really didn't put too much stock on doing anything else at Sunday's picnic but he was using his reluctance with obvious adult disdain for my earlier put downs.

"Okay, we'll bring our bottles to school Friday and hide them in the bush behind the barn. Then we'll be all ready to demolish them when the time is ripe."

"Great," said Albert. We shook hands sealing once again our indissoluble friendship.

Friday seemed to take forever to come. By Thursday afternoon's recess Albert and I were so full of anticipating the weekend's excitement that we could barely contain ourselves. During the last class before recess we were exchanging little notes across the aisle bearing inscriptions like, "Tomorrow the treasure is hid; one day buried and raised on the third day," and "It's a matter of time and new worlds will open up before us." Albert was a fairly good artist and he handed me a folded paper on which was a pencil drawing of a goddess-like figure drinking from an upturned Graecian vase. It was difficult to keep our attention on what Mr. Thompson was writing on the blackboard. Our older brothers, Doug, the one who threw manure on me, and Jack, Albert's older brother, eyed us suspiciously and nodded to each other knowingly. We enjoyed this interplay because it signified at last our growing seniority in the little school which in another year or two would see us as the adult guarantors.

At recess we were the first out the door. We ran down to the school barn, rounded the far corner and vanished into the shrubs and bushes behind it.

"Let's hide it here next to this black poplar" said Albert as we scratched around for a good site where tomorrow morning we'd deposit our two bottles well before the school bell.

"That's good", I replied. But maybe we should bring in a couple of rocks to mark the spot. You know how one tree looks like another when you're sure you know the spot."

We scuffled around under the trees looking for stones. We had a hunch our older brothers might be on the lookout for us so we didn't want to give our positions away be being seen outside the bush. It took us the full recess period to organize the site of tomorrow's treasure hiding.

The eye of God certainly loomed over me the next morning as I prepared to leave for school rather earlier than usual. Not since running to school with the other guys in search of tokens and mementos of the dance the night before had I left this early. Because there was no reason for leaving before the others today Mother was curious.

"Why are you in such a hurry?" she asked. I felt the unseen penetration from above as I with mouth going a little dry replied,

"Oh, uh, Albert and I got this thing to do in preparation for Sunday's picnic. I'm not sure what Mr. Thompson wants us to do but we said we'd come early."

"Oh," said Mother, "it's funny he didn't mention to me when I stopped by last night that he was getting you and Albert to help. How nice." I felt like dropping the whole project now, but Albert would never let me forget it. I started off for school the usual way and then skirted around the back of the yard and entered the bush, where our toilet was, from the far side. Quickly I scooped up the aspirin bottle, stuck it in my lunch bag, and retreated on the same elusive path. I was off like a deer.

Albert was already in position near the black poplar. He had scooped up a fair bit of ground and leaf mold with a stick and his bottle lay shining in the rays of the sun breaking through the foliage at the base of the hole.

"Did you have any trouble?" he asked.

"Why should I?" I responded. I didn't feel like going over with him the discomfiting brief interview with my Mother and the resurgence of criminal feelings I encountered when the eye of God pierced my body.

"I went out last night and hid my bottle near the side of the road so that I wouldn't have to sneak around the yard this morning," he said as if sensing some of my uneasiness.

I set my bottle next to his and we covered the spot. We took the two rocks and set them one on top of the other over the disturbed earth. Our mission was completed. Now we had to wait out one more day of school, all day Saturday and half of Sunday before we could return to this site and enjoy the fruits of our long-planned endeavor.

There wasn't too much that occurred of an academic nature that day in school as far as Albert and I were concerned. We assumed the stance of two wise men who rose above menial tasks and projects in the room. The day was spent largely in passing clever notes, exchanging meaningful glances and generally acting oblivious of the rest of the kids. It was a particularly good day for doing something which was above the attention and understanding of our two older brothers.

Saturday's chores were like so many necessary evils to get out of the way. The hours seemed longer than usual. The span between breakfast and dinner seemed endless as I asked my Dad or my brother the time. Doug, finally flabbergasted by this persistence, chastised me as he lifted a forkful of hay,

"For heaven's sake, how many times are you going to ask the time? What's the difference anyway? What've you got, some great plan or something, eh? Maybe you and Albert are going to blow up the world or something at six o'clock maybe!" I decided not to ask the time anymore that weekend.

Sunday dawned still, cloudless and serene. Meadowlarks and robins welcomed the new week. It was much easier than usual to hop out of bed when called and get dressed to pursue the round of pre-breakfast yard chores. Even the cows seemed more co-operative than usual as I rounded them up in the pasture and headed them towards the barn.

Mom prepared bacon and eggs. The aroma of fresh, perked coffee, frying side bacon inundated the fresh morning air. It encouraged efficiency in the barns and the chicken house. I ate a hearty breakfast. Conversation came around to the day's activities.

"Guess I'll walk to the picnic today," Doug was saying. "Jack and I are supposed to help set up ball diamonds."

"Can I come with you?" I asked. "Albert will likely go with Jack."

"We've already cleared that, brat," he said in his usual loving manner. "Jack and I are to look after this alone. You guys come along and get sloshing around and nobody gets anything done."

"Okay, okay," I acted hurt, "I'll help Dad around here and go with them. Somebody's got to take responsibility, right?" I didn't really mind. When you're in a euphoric mood little things like personal taunts and scurrilous remarks don't bother much.

We drove into the Banner Hall grounds with several other carloads. The country roads in both directions were marked with a rising cloud of grey dust that hovered in the air. The day was sticky and hot. Disembarking from the back seat I spotted Albert near the booth. He was wearing neatly pressed long pants, a clean sport shirt and running shoes. His black hair was oiled and parted neatly. It occurred to me again that the two of us were getting rather tall and good-looking

"Hi guy!" I poked him in the arm muscle.

"Hi yourself!" he returned the gesture. Hitting each other in the back portion of the muscle of the upper arm is a kind of painful nudge of brotherhood. It's a sign of deep friendship between growing boys.

"Things are getting ready to happen," I said and with hands in my back pockets casually surveyed the various activities. Truckloads of ball players were descending on the ball diamonds at the far end of the large yard; some men were marking off race tracks for the footraces; women were carrying boilers full of hot water and coffee which lapped over the edges, into the booth next to us. A man with a half ton truck was wrestling ice cream barrels to the ground. Conversation, laughter and shouted greetings filled the air. All of it held a special kind of expectancy for each of us right then.

"Yeah, it should be a very good day," Albert replied. "I guess you and I are going to view the world from a little different place today," he said philosophically.

"Gosh, Albert, I can hardly wait. When do you think we can hit into the bush?" I responded, my voice cracking a bit with the excitement.

"Maybe in a few minutes. Maybe we should kind of stroll around all over so that everybody can see we're here and won't miss us. They'll sort of expect that we'll be in one of the other groups."

"Good idea," I said. "Let's get strolling." Our pace quickened as we moved around. We didn't linger very long as we feigned interest in what the little groups of people were doing. We'd ask a few questions like, "Who's going to play on this diamond first?" and "Are there going to be three-legged races today?" Most of the time we didn't hang around for the answers since the people didn't seem too interested in us anyway.

We walked clean around the yard to the edge of the school yard near the north end of the barn. We walked around the front of the barn and entered the bush on the south side where we wouldn't be seen by anybody at the picnic. Now we would taste of forbidden fruit.

Both of us got down on our knees and started to scrape out the loose earth after we threw the two rocks aside. The soil was mixed with rotting leaves and it was easy to scoop out. In the next second or so we'd have the bottles in our hands. We'd unscrew the caps and down the contents like two old cronies celebrating a naval victory with flasks of rum. The world would begin to dance before our eyes and we'd see visions and shout prophecies at the sky.

But as we scooped out the remaining loose earth we discovered that our cache had been stolen. The bottles were gone! In the two little creases that lay parallel to each other at the base of the hole was a paper rolled up with an elastic around it. With sinking hearts we snapped the band off the roll and unfurled the page. There printed across it were the words:

"You stupid nuts! Don't you know that vanilla could kill you? Lucky we got wind of what you were doing. We've dumped it out and smashed the bottles. We won't tell if you don't ask,

Your loving brothers,
Doug and Jack

The eye of God became a little kinder that moment.

SWIMMING HOLE HOPES

A desire to test the effects of vanilla with Albert was not the only yearning my adolescent body was feeling as the eighth grade was drawing to a conclusion. Physically and psychologically we had grown a lot since our episodes with Corny and his pornographic material and our musings about some of the happenings during the night life at Banner Hall. The girls, whose scrawny, bony frames we found disgusting and whose incessant whispering and giggling in our presence merely annoyed us, began to take on intriguing characteristics.

For some reason we began to tease the girls with a little more vigour. Pulling their hair and tormenting them almost to tears was always good clean sport. 'Til this time there were no added feelings to this fun; girls were like so many unwanted pets, you could hurt them if you wanted to, but it didn't do that much for you if you did. It was a matter of tolerating them when we had to be in the same room, using them for a bit of play and then skipping out on them or bugging them until they were scared away so that we could get on with really interesting things. As spring and summer heralded the wonderful promise of summer vacation, Albert and I began to talk more about girls. Somehow we tried to put into words the awareness we both felt that the sort of feelings that were barely hinted at when we followed Helen around earlier that year were taking shape within us. We noticed that we were talking about the older girls in our room. We were actually referring to them by their names! Chicken Grease gradually became Phyllis; Longnose took on her real name, Mary, and Redface whose blush gave her that name, as we discovered we really liked that trait, became her real self, Dorothy. And on it went. The girls of Runneberg who were in Grade 7 below us and Grade 9 above us began to take on individuality in our sight.

I was alerted to this change in my attention one day whilst walking in the school barn with Albert and some of the kids at the afternoon recess.

"Let's play tag!" challenged Katie, who was always Longlegs to me. She was one of the taller Grade 7 girls and her slim, rather lanky body was beginning to fill out in fetching places. I felt a gentle surge of warmth run through me as she tugged at my sleeve. We ran along together laughing and pushing and shoving. I enjoyed observing how when she ran her loose fitting blouse bobbed in and out gently where her tiny breasts were taking shape. There was no gentleness in my nudges and jabs though as I engaged in the kind of non-verbal communication that is a kind of warm-up exercise in human relations at this stage of puberty.

"Okay, kid, you're it!" I shoved her hard enough to make her stumble and almost fall. We had run clear of the other kids and were jostling each other towards one side of the schoolyard. Clearly on the outside it was plain that we were engaging in a kind of feud, but from somewhere within us, at least speaking for myself, there was a sense of friendliness and camaraderie. I had a wish, a desire in fact, to trip her and fall to the ground with her but somehow felt a little reservation about doing so. This was unlike my former treatment of girls in a situation where'd we come into bodily contact. Then I'd seek to apply some hurt, but today I just wanted to play around.

"You're it yourself" she came back hard. I took the hard blow of her fist into my arm muscle. It felt good.

"Not so smart!" I responded with a belt across her shoulder. She ran free for a few steps and faltered just a little, I caught up to her and executed a neat spin around her just out of reach. Then I started running backwards.

"I can keep away from you running like this; look, I can even run faster backwards with my eyes closed!" Enticed by my teasing, she ran towards me, her arms straight out ahead of her body. With both hands she lunged into my front and I lost my balance with a little help from my wishes and the two of us fell to the ground; I was underneath and she was across me. With screams of pretended torment the two of us rolled around on the ground. I dug my fingers into her sides beneath her elbows and tickled; she screeched in uncontrolled response to my vigorous tickling. Gradually, not too quickly, we separated, got up and brushed the grass and dust off our clothes. I was intrigued by the good feeling that accompanied this horseplay. Katie's laughter and mine subsided in intensity as we got to our feet. Obviously we were both reflecting on the momentary glow that our bodies ignited in each other as they rubbed together. It was enough to cope with at this moment. We walked away from each other. She to a group of girls by the girls' toilet and I to where Albert was picking up toadstools and crushing them between his hands.

"Albert, have you ever noticed how some of those girls aren't nearly as miserable as they used to be?" I asked, picking up a mangled toadstool.

"Yeah, I've also noticed how you and Katie like playing tag," he responded. "If is kind of different now though, isn't it? Yesterday, Phyllis and I were "it" during hide and seek. Like we're supposed to, we went inside the barn to count before calling "Ready" and we kind of shoved each other around a bit. Sort of the same as you and Katie were doing just now. I noticed that I didn't get mad this time. We even forgot to count, so I just came out and hollered 'Ready', but it must have taken longer than if we'd been counting." I picked up some more stems and pieces of toadstools and squashed them into a ball which I heaved in baseball pitching style against the side of the barn. It seemed to me that we were thinking the same thoughts but we didn't know how to verbalize them.

We ran towards the school in response to the vigorous ringing of the school bell by Mr. Thompson.

As the days approached June exams, there was an obvious increase in the number of times that Albert and I got mixed up in boy-girl games. Even the greatly cherished games like softball and dodge ball seemed like more fun when the girls played with us. Now, instead of eating our lunches on the other side of the school from the girls we often opened our pails within talking distance and certainly within shooting distance for tossing orange peelings and balls of waxed paper in their direction.

Albert and I were in the mood to explore our new found interest in more depth. We indicated to each other one day on the way home from school that these chance meetings with the opposite sex were not satisfying enough. We'd like to set up something where we could nourish our curiosity and our growing awareness of the unique qualities of girls in a way that would satisfy our pangs of hunger without getting us into situations we wouldn't understand. The conversation got around to discussing shapes and figures.

"Did you notice how when Mary was up at the blackboard today her dress shaped kind of round at her hips when she was writing?" I asked. "I wonder why girls' bottoms are shaped the way they are. Mary's really developing a shape there. When she walked away from the blackboard, honestly, I though I'd swallow my pencil; she kind of waddled and wiggled in a way that made it look as if she was wrapped in slices of calf's liver."

"It's like Helen," said Albert, "they're all copying her. She walks like that and these girls want to be like her in looks anyway. It wasn't Mary that got me so much as Dorothy. When Mr. Thompson asked her to get up in front and read from her French she got all red like she always does, except her blushing is really getting cute. I noticed her smile cut through her rosy lips like peppermints lined up for eating. If she ever flashes that smile at me I'm telling you I'll blush all over my body like she does in her face."

"Katie's breasts are really getting huge," I confided. "If she forgets to button her blouse up someday they'll be flapping in the wind. And Phyllis' hair drives me out of my mind. Sitting behind her in school is like trying to concentrate on arithmetic when the Lone Ranger is on. Only worse."

"I wonder what it'd be like to really see these gals as they really are," Albert blurted. "I mean suppose you and I could actually see them through their clothes the way they're made. I wonder if they'd actually look like some of Corny's pictures. Remember that girl and that guy. Gee, when we looked at those last summer I thought Corny was sort of crazy. But remember how he said he figured he was doing us a favor showing them to us and telling us about feelings we'd have some day? Well, the way I figure it, we've come quite a ways to what he was talking about."

"Let's think of some way that we can get a look at them without actually having to sneak up to their houses or something," I suggested. "You know, there's got to be some respectable way of seeing them without getting into trouble with our parents and everything."

"How about a swim in the old swimming hole?" Albert asked.

"Sure," I mocked, "just go up tomorrow after lunch and say, 'Okay, girls, it's off to the swimming hole! Let's go! Last one in's a frog." Albert looked disgusted with my attempt at humor. He kicked a chunk of dried mud into the ditch. I scampered after it and picked it up and heaved at a blackbird sitting on the telephone wire. The bird flew away.

"Don't get mad, Albert. Maybe you got an idea. How could we get them swimming down there? At least when we'd be around?"

The boys from Runneberg often used the noon hours of early summer for a skinny dip in Petresky's dugout. It was located about a half mile south of the school not too far from the road but a good distance from their yard. It was a water hole for their livestock. Because it was set into a deep ravine, the spring runoff and the June rains kept the water quite fresh. It was accessible and the bushes gave good cover for removing our clothes.

"We'll have a contest between the boys and girls," he said with relish. "We've got to work it in a way that they'll know they're not being watched when they're swimming, but also in a way that they've got to compete. You know how girls are when they think maybe the boys are doing better than they are? We'll get them thinking that we think we're better swimmers than they are. We'll get them in an argument or something, then make them think it's all their idea." I was impressed with Albert's ability to put things together in his mind once he got the initial idea.

"Tomorrow when we're having lunch we'll get talking about it, okay? But before we bring it up let's get to the other guys first. Maybe we can see them before school and at recess." The plan was taking shape as we walked more briskly along the road. We got to Albert's gate, said "See yah," to each other and I continued down the road alone with my imagination leaping ahead of me. I wondered if Dorothy's blush ran all the way down her back.

The other guys in the class weren't difficult to talk to about our plan. They pledged their fullest co-operation. We'd talk it up a lot at noon about our prowess in swimming and about how it's too bad that God made boys so much more athletic than girls but that they'd just have to accept the fact that they weren't water people.

The noon hour's arrival was chimed by pushing the button on the little silver bell that sat on Mr. Thompson's desk. We all left the room with our lunch pails. It was too hot to sit inside so we lined up along the west side of the school with our backs against the wall. The short shadows of high noon left our feet in the sunlight.

Raymond had a good-sized voice. He wasn't the school bully but he worked at trying to be. It was usually good to have him on your side if there was going to be trouble. Today, of course, the trouble would be verbal and we knew even if the girls didn't know yet, that the boys would be all sticking together.

"That was some swim yesterday," he boomed, "it's getting pretty tough to pick a winner. "Funny how us guys are just about all equal when it comes to swimming. Y'know I was reading the other day that boys are more athletic than girls when it comes to this sort of thing. They've got more drive and aren't scared of jumping into water holes and stuff which makes them better physical beings." That was a very provocative statement to make in front of a group of females even back in the '40's. A couple of the girls looked as though they were going to speak but the guys were well-organized. The original idea may have belonged to Albert and me, but as was so often the case when the action got going we got left out of the front lines. Henry got up on his feet and faced the group lining the west wall.

"Ray's right," he said, "there's a big difference between boys and girls. Not just in those plain things like body build and stuff, but in the down deep areas like real strength of mind and will. We know what 'guts' are because as boys and men we're the group who's called upon to stand up for what's right and put down what's wrong. That's why when you think of soldiers and fighters, you normally think of men. I guess it goes right back to who really has the nerve to do things like diving into water holes and stuff." I thought it was maybe a little obvious the way these two fellows brought in the water hole reference both times, but then who is to evaluate the naivete of a competitive woman?

"Yeah, he's right," I murmured but couldn't think of anything else to say. It seemed funny that Albert and I could verbalize this tremendous plan in each other's company but sure seemed helpless in getting it off the ground here. We needed these other guys.

Tony got to his feet and stood at the opposite end of the line facing Henry. "Look, it's easy enough to figure out. It's plain that the boys from this school are more daring, more brave, and willing to try more things than the girls. And because that's the way it is here, it must be that way all over the world. I was reading that that's why women like black women in Africa and those places all end up doing the dirty work around the yard and everything; the boys and men are smarter and also willing to lose their lives for the kids and the sissy women. It's no different any place in the world." With that kind of universal sweep, he neatly dealt the small group of older girls a pretty strong blow. The well-timed speeches and the semi-belligerent manner of delivery were hitting the mark. Dorothy jumped to her feet, face crimson red, blushing more than when she was put on the spot in class by Mr. Thompson.

"Listen you phonies. You're talking up a storm if you want one. What are you trying to do, make us look like a bunch of whimpering puppies or something? If it wasn't for the girls of this school we'da lost the last ball game to Fairland. Who was pitching and catching? Girls, that's who!" It was a pretty effective rebuttal. That game last Friday dampened our spirits a bit because it's true as Dorothy said the two guys who were the starting pitcher and catcher got pulled by Mr. Thompson in favor of the two girls who did in fact come through to win the game. I got thinking about this and was kind of in sympathy with the point she made, when Raymond got to his feet and got the conversation back to swimming holes.

"Okay, Dorothy, redden down a little. Sure you've proven that you can play ball sometimes, maybe in a pinch. But we're talking about general things like real strength. For example, all us guys can swim two lengths of Petrosky's dugout, and with all our clothes off! You know," he bluffed, "anybody can swim better in the comfort of a bathing suit. But we guys, right here," he pointed at all of us, Albert and I felt proud, "we can whip out there after school any day and strip off our clothes, dive in one end, whip up the length and return without even looking up. All of us. Every one of us." He paused just a second and came in with the clincher, "How about you?"

Mary was on her feet, followed by Katie and Phyllis. It took another second for some of the younger ones to follow but they did. The older girls were emphatic. Mary began to say "We'll race you guys on anything anywhere . . ." and Phyllis interrupted, "We'll go out there today, after school, we'll have our own little swimming party, and just you see who's got the strength and the guts!"

The younger girls of the school backed away and looked as if they were getting ready to go swinging or something. But we had these older ones hooked.

"Tell you what," interjected Raymond, "if you girls are really serious about this, you of course won't want us there to check you. Especially if we're going to keep this fair and everything, you'll want to swim as we always do without any clothes on to help you along. I guess what we could do is wait here at the school. You girls go and run through the contest and then you come back and tell us how you did. We'd have to trust you though as to whether you're telling a fib or anything." Of course, we didn't care anything about whether they were able to swim at all. We just wanted to pretend we'd be waiting for the results, but we'd be hiding in the bushes at the far end of the dugout. These could be reached by heading around to the back of a steep hill, crawling over the hill and hanging in those bushes which covered the dugout side of the hill.

"Trust us!" Mary exclaimed. "Who's to trust who? You guys are just big-mouthing your great accomplishments. You maybe could tell a few fibs too, eh?" She didn't push the point beyond that. Raymond could see the possible direction the accusation might take, so he quickly picked up on the former course.

"We'll stay after school and bat the ball around and stuff. We'll give you guys three quarters of an hour. Shouldn't take any longer than that. Don't forget we guys got a lot of chores and stuff to do at home to keep it nice for you girls! You hurry back here and tell us how many drowned and we'll come and pull out the bodies." It was well-aimed.

"Right after school, big mouths!" shouted Dorothy. "We'll be back before you even get started batting the ball. It doesn't take us all day to go through a child's game."

We packed up our lunch pails and moved off into little groups. The bigger boys went off laughing and talking. We'd wait for the girls to head down the road then we'd cut across Reid's field, swing around behind the hill and feast our eyes on the puberty-swelling bodies of our female colleagues. Dumb women, you could talk them into almost anything.

After school the smaller kids picked up their lunch pails and books and headed for home. We older boys pretended to get ready for some ball practice. We got out the bats, gloves and a couple of softballs. The older girls were now militant. They must have been passing notes and communicating their thoughts about this endeavor in school because they were off like so many shots down the road towards the dugout. In a matter of a few minutes they were out of sight and we slipped through the barbed wire fence of Reid's oat field. It was easy to stay pretty well hidden from anyone who might be checking on our whereabouts. The oats were high and we trekked through them to the base of a ravine that followed along a row of sloping hills to the tall hill which was our objective.

"Albert and I ran close together. "Gosh," he puffed, "think of it. We dreamed this whole thing up and look what it's come to in such a short time."

"Its's fabulous," I puffed in return, trying to pull my right foot free of a pigweed that wound around it, "If it's this easy to set a thing like this up, imagine what we can do in the future."

The oatfield ran into a grass-filled gully that veered to the right as we approached the steep hill. We scrambled along the base of this gully and crouched close to the ground as we started up the sharp incline. The top of the hill was ridged with low shrubs which hung over the other side. It would be necessary to hang onto the scraggy trunks and branches of these trees while watching the girls so as not to slip down the bank into the dugout. We slithered on our stomachs over the top so that our feet would precede us downwards. The shrubs were well-clothed in greenery. We'd have to maneuver ourselves into positions that would allow us to see through the leaves without actually disclosing our presence.

Excited female voices could be heard somewhere below us and at the opposite end of the dugout. The girls must be in the taller bushes down there taking off their clothes. Albert and I stayed fairly close to one another.

"Wonder who'll be the first to hit the water?" I whispered across to him. His face showed the exertion of having difficulty getting into a comfortable position which would free us at the same time to enjoy an unobstructed view.

"I dunno," he replied, "will likely be Dorothy. She was the maddest. She'll likely come flying through those trees any moment. Boy, imagine the view."

"Wow!" he responded, "Can't really wait much longer."

There was more talk and a lot of giggling going on. The girls had obviously forgotten that they were angry. They sounded as if they were actually enjoying the experience of getting ready for a skinny dip.

"Just like girls," said Albert, "Talking a mile a minute. Next thing you know they'll forget what they came here for."

"Females, shemales," I muttered disgustedly.

There were whoops of laughter now coming up from below. I imagine that they were looking at each other's bodies and reacting. Albert was thinking the same thing which he revealed by, "Probably just noticed Katie's hangouts!" in a rather loud whisper. I started to giggle and slipped a little.

The shrub I was hanging on to began showing signs of losing its rather tenuous grip into mother earth. I could see imminent disaster so I reached over and grabbed onto the tree Albert was placing his weight on.

"Get off of here," he said with some exasperation in his voice, "The whole thing'll let go!"

"Albert, for God's sake, I'm slipping, help me," I retorted, grabbing his shrub in desperation.

It didn't give us any further warning. The roots of Albert's tree pulled out like a wild mustard plant coming out of summerfallow. Down we went. Two trees in hand, feet slithering over the little pebbles and chunks of grass that jutted off the cliff-like hill. There was no graceful way to enter that water. We hit full impact of our bodies going under and then bobbing up like a couple of corks. Letting go of the trees, we commenced swimming to the opposite shore where a gentle slope would be our only exit right into the group of jeering, fully clothed girls who added pain to our injury with words like,

"We knew all the time. Bigmouths! Little boys wanted to see what little girls look like! Well here we are; come and look at us!

It's hard to be a hero.

GRADUATION

Albert and I couldn't quite figure out why everyone wanted to make such a big deal out of the fact that we had completed Grade 8. The exams were over and Mr. Thompson had handed out the report cards. I knew I'd be back in Runneberg again in the fall because that was pretty much what happened to anyone who wanted to go on to "higher" education. You enrolled in the province's correspondence course and worked out of the same one room school you occupied for the previous eight years. But Grade eight graduation still marked a watershed of kinds.

Although I was to be the only one of the five eighth graders staying on, I didn't associate too much glory with that. Albert and the other guys chose the option of concluding their formal education at this stage and going full-time farming. I chose, with the encouragement of my parents, the less romantic route of sticking at school at least for another year or so. The one big consolation to this as I could foresee it would be that I'd be one of the biggest boys in school. Now that the older girls didn't look all that bad I realized I might have a pretty open field in that department.

Passing from public school life had to be marked by some sort of ritual. Mr. Thompson and some of the parents had been arranging an appropriate departure ceremony. There was to be a strictly school function on the Friday afternoon of the last day of school followed in the evening by a sort of potluck supper involving all the school kids and their parents. Albert and I could see the first event, but we balked at the idea of the second. It seemed silly to bring in our parents for something as anti-climatic as marking the closing of the school year. Besides, we'd get all the ice cream and cake we could eat at the kids' party.

The afternoon party came and went in an uneventful atmosphere. We were, somehow, a different group that afternoon. Especially the five of us. In one way we'd become very old. Mr. Thompson didn't seem that much our senior. The young kids suddenly appeared very young and immature. Although Albert and I had decided ahead of time that we'd really gorge ourselves on the sweets offered as a farewell toast, we, in fact, exercised a mature restraint. The conversation was less frivolous than we had hoped, but it was us who made it that way. We were more like polite middle-aged people discussing the economics of the day without delving too deeply into the subject lest they become controversial, than children at a windup school party.

I guess there was through that day an underlying feeling that some long-lasting relationships were about to be gently severed. The greatest dream a fellow could conceive of was to look forward to that last day of public school. But now it was painfully present. Albert and I and the others had gone through a pile of living together in that little world. Now the world was about to become a lot larger. How could we cope with our new world without the support of those who knew us best? Each of us would be doing things much more on our own than ever before. After the second helping of ice cream sat too long in our stomachs and the subdued chatter got around to practical things like how we'd clean up our desks and get the room in order for tonight's supper, our group broke up and we headed, rather dejectedly, for home.

I didn't really object to mother's insistence that for tonight's occasion I wear a white shirt and tie, pressed pants and polished shoes. Normally this kind of garb was reserved for a church service or some other formal and boring affair. And normally I fought tooth and nail against this imposition on my individual human rights knowing all the time that my arguments would get me nowhere except a further scolding. The mood of this Friday in my life was different. The fight had gone. There was within me, and I suspect within my colleagues, ambivalent feelings. I had reached a point in life idealized in many conversations and dreams but now devoid of the glamor and excitement cherished in those dreams. Albert and I in a very real way would be parting. I couldn't get my feelings around this realization. Certainly there would be great encounters we'd share in the future at the community dances and the picnics. But the joy would be diminished, maybe even shattered because so much of the relish came in the planning, the talking through prior to the events and the imagined heroism we imputed to ourselves. Now I'd be alone.

The potluck supper was a gourmet's success. Albert's mother had prepared the best headcheese stew of her life. Raymond's mother brought a potful of Hungarian goulash like I'd never tasted. An assortment of Canadianized ethnic dishes from Germany, Hungary, Poland, the Ukraine and Scotland brought tremendous temporary relief to the nostalgia lurking just behind our Adam's apples. Mr. Thompson's speech about citizenship and community involvement impressed us.

GRADUATION

He was at his best. I was real proud to be a Runneberg school graduate as he sat down to the applause of the assembled parents and students. I felt for a while that all the unknown details of the future could not be too overwhelming. When we were introduced then as eighth grade grads we actually rose to the swelling pride within us. It seemed kind of ridiculous, these introductions, because everyone knew more about each of us than anyone could tell in an hour's speech, nevertheless there was an air of propriety about the procedure.

We had moved the desks earlier in the day into two big circles. Adults and kids straddled the desks balancing their large dinner plates and other utensils on the narrow tops. It was a friendly, informal setting with an aura of importance over everything because of the speech, the introductions and our better clothing. When the introductions were finished, people relaxed in easy conversation over dessert and coffee. Then while the adults packed up dishes in preparation for a whist game, we kids left the classroom and moved off into little groups and pairs in the schoolyard. Albert and I went down to the school barn and sat on a log in the shade of the east side, not too far from the old tree under which we had hid the vanilla bottles in one of our heroic escapades.

"Whatcha gonna do tomorrow?" I broke a rather disturbing silence.

"Oh, Dad wants me to get started harrowing the summerfallow east of the tracks," he replied. "I guess now that school's all over I've got to take up some of the work waiting there for me." He paused. I was silent. Then he continued, "Sure will be great; no more books, no more homework. Just farming every day."

"Yeah, sure will be," I said half-heartedly. We couldn't think of anything else to say for awhile.

"Look at that stupid meadowlark chasing that crow," I pointed at the two birds spiralling through the air above us. It was a familiar sight actually and didn't deserve any comment because we'd witnessed this kind of natural display for survival since we were kids.

"Yeah," replied Albert, "sure shows a lot of spunk." More silence. "School's sure going to be great come fall, "I said. "Just think of me once in awhile, will you? I'll be turning off correspondence courses in the morning and flirting around with all the girls in the afternoon. Teacher won't look at me like I'm some kid. I'll sort of be my own boss." I figured maybe this would get some conversation going like it used to.

"Who you going to tell about all the things you're going to do and then don't," answered wise old Albert. "How many great old swimming hole experiences you going to dream up all by yourself?"

"Gee, it's going to be different all right. Maybe somehow we can get together just to talk about things like this. You know, you can't harrow all the time; maybe I'll meet you out there or you can come over to the school yard and we can catch up on some of the really exciting things of life." There was nostalgia and pathos mixed in my attempt at meeting the new lifestyle.

"Remember, pal, how we laughed at and made fun of old Hank for coming back with his team of horses when we were playing ball after school last fall? Yet old Hank had just quit the year before. He's not that much older than we are right now. But because he wasn't at school, we didn't want him plowing into our group. Y'know that must've seemed mean to Hank. I'll bet he would have liked it a lot better if we'd made him feel like he was one of us. But we didn't. And, y'know, that'll be me come fall." Albert's voice cracked just a little and he concentrated on a clump of grass he had rooted out by kicking his heel into the ground.

"Albert, listen," I tried to counter the pleading tone in my voice, "It's not that way with us. We got too much going. We can't just figure that because you're farming and I'm studying that everything's going to be changed. We'll phone each other like we do now," we customarily rang each other on the party line a few minutes after school, "and we'll keep up on each other's ideas and stuff. It's too scary to think of not keeping going on that kind of connection. There's a lot of new things we can do together."

"Sure," said Albert sardonically, "I'll run in from the field or the barn or whatever when you come from school just to pick up on all the day's happenings. I can just see what great successes we're both going to be. No, I think likely we're coming to the end of something that wasn't as bad as we sometimes made it out to be. All the times we talked about finishing school and getting on to real living may have just been a way of not facing up to some of the real things that were happening. It's going to be different, I guess. Somehow we'll keep in touch though." His voice filtered out its energy. He seemed so much older.

"You bet we'll keep in touch, " I replied. "We got too much going not to."

Someone was calling that the whist drive was about to start. We got up slowly and walked toward the school.